Snook

By DC Fidler

Published by DCFidler Publishing

2024

Published by DCFidler Publishing
300 West Fifth Street #647
Charlotte, NC 28202

DCFidlerpublishing@gmail.com

Printed in the United States of America
by Kindle Direct Publishing

12, 11, 10, 9, 8, 7, 6, 5, 4, 3

Cover art: by Donald Carl Fidler

WGAW Registration: 2273796
Library of Congress Registration: 1-14308743101

ISBN: (paperback) 979-8-9904735-7-7
ISBN: (ebook) 979-8-9904735-8-4

Appreciation

Thank you to my wonderful writing teachers: Doris Betts, Max Steele, Wallace Kaufman, and writers-in-residence James Dickey and Robert Anderson at the University of North Carolina at Chapel Hill. That was decades ago, but your caring presences continue to instruct me.

Thank you to Sandi Constantino-Thompson for your wonderful lessons about editing and your infectious enthusiasm that keeps me writing and rewriting long hours each day.

Thank you to RJ Casey, Andrew Trumbull, Ben Hogan, Paul Rashid, and Travis Teffner, my sometimes co-writers and writing consultants, who are consistently my audience when I write solo.

Thank you to my numerous restaurant and coffee-shop buddies who nourish me with food as well as nourish me with enthusiasm for writing.

Thank you to the Charlotte Writers Club for the many writing classes and critiques from club writers.

Snook

SNOOK

By DC Fidler

1. IN GOD WE TRUST

Eight-year-old Snook heard her mother shriek.

She froze for a moment, tiptoed to her bedroom door, opened it wider, leaned into the hall, and listened.

All was quiet. Maybe problems of the world had resolved.

Her mother shouted, "Jessie Rae Tate."

Snook raced to her bed, reached beneath it, and pulled out a frayed cardboard shoebox. Her freshly-caught field mouse had escaped. Where was Twinkles? Had her cat, Mr. Gammon, cornered Twinkles? Ripped her little body apart?

Her mother yelled her full legal name again.

Snook knew that when her mother yelled her nickname, a meal was ready. When she yelled Snook's first and middle names, there would be questions about minor issues. But yelling her full name?

Snook carted the shoebox to the bathroom and crawled on her knees. "Where is she?"

Her mother frowned through a mask of cold cream. "How do you know that thing's a she?"

"She's pregnant."

"Lord have mercy, child. What terrible sin did I commit to deserve such treatment?"

Snook pictured the dozen or so "uncles" who had stayed at their house, each for months at a time, claiming they were planning to marry Eliza Tate, but disappearing as the date for matrimony approached. "I don't know, Mama. I don't recall you ever sinning."

"Nothing that God or I know about. That's for sure."

"For sure Mama." Snook peeked behind the toilet.

"Not behind there." Eliza nodded toward a pile of folded towels on the floor. "That thing scampered behind my clean towels. I can't watch. My heart won't handle witnessing that wicked rodent again."

Snook rested her chest on the cotton-towel tower and reached behind it. "There you are, Twinkles."

Eliza glanced at Snook in the mirror. "Don't offer your face to that creature. He'll bite your nose off."

"She. And no, she won't. She slept on my pillow next to my face most of the night."

"I can't take this." Eliza fled the room crying.

Snook assessed the drama was her mother's usual fake crying. She snuggled Twinkles against her cheek. "Me and you'll be fine."

She eased Twinkles into her box and sealed the lid with cellophane tape at each end.

Snook stood before her cracked dressing mirror and stared past herself, seeing faces of her third-fourth-and-fifth grade classmates as she rehearsed her show-and-tell presentation.

"Good afternoon, Miss Bushby and classmates. My life story. I was born Jessie Rae Tate in 1951 here in Winding Gulf, West Virginia to Frederik and Eliza Tate. When I was two, Daddy was killed in Korea a week before that war ended. People say they sense my daddy down in the mines protecting them, sometimes seeing him outta the side of their eyes.

Daddy gave me my nickname: Snook. All I can find in the dictionary about Snook is that it means mucous.

When I turned three, *God* was added to the Pledge of Allegiance. When I turned six, *In God We Trust* was added to American paper money. Mama says money minted earlier is sinful money. She allows me a God-blessed one-dollar-silver-certificate bill to be taped to my mirror.

When I grow up, I'm gonna be a veterinarian, cause I love all animals great and small.

That is my life story. Thank you for your kind attention."

Snook winked in the mirror at herself. "Good job, Snook Tate."

Her mother yelled from the kitchen, "Snook? You coming to breakfast? Your egg is getting cold."

"Yes ma'am. Soon as I find my other shoe."

2. KEEP OUT

On weekends, Snook typically rose an hour early, inhaled a piece of white bread smothered in grape jelly, and was out the door to ride her bike to Epperly Hill to spy on folks living in fancy houses, browse the company store, or scale the Camp Two train trestle. But today was special. She planned to traipse up the hillside behind their unpainted house, enter the thick woods, follow a dirt road grown-over enough to be a foot path, and drag along her seven-year-old friend Olsen Nielsen. Although she thought of Olsen as being wimpy, she assessed his arms were strong and her goal for the day required such.

Olsen was inches taller than Snook. She assessed his height was due to his oversized head. She once drew attention to that fact and Olsen defended himself. "Grandmommie says that like my father, the rest of my body will surge and catch up with my head." Snook held her tongue, resolved that Olsen's protruding belly had already surged.

As Snook predicted, Olsen's potbelly undermined his hill-climbing heartiness, requiring frequent stops to catch his breath, making excuses he wanted to watch a butterfly or take-in the beauty of an orange Turk's Cap Lily. He twice spotted praying mantises that he required sitting on logs to study.

After a hike that took long enough that Snook felt she could have jogged to Wyoming County and back, they reached their destination: a steeply slanted baseball-field-size clearing. At the opposite end, in a cave mouth at the bottom of a hill, *Keep Out* was painted in blood-red letters on weather-worn boards.

Still panting, Olsen squatted on a rock coated with orange dust. "What is that?"

Snook shrugged *no big deal.* "A cave. Maybe an old mine. An old Cherokee or Civil-War or bank-robber hideout. I want to discover what."

Snook shielded her eyes from sunlight and peered through one of many gaps in the haphazardly nailed planks.

Olsen was still panting and speaking with punctuated gasps. "What can you see?"

"Black." Snook tugged on a board and it yielded an inch, creaking like a rusty-door hinge.

"What are you doing? It says *keep out.*"

"I want to see why it says *keep out.*"

Olsen slapped his forehead. "You're crazy, Snook Tate. Keep out means it's dangerous."

"Or hiding secrets."

"Like dragons or rattlers."

"Come help me pull on this board."

Olsen stared at his feet, watching one foot wiggle as if an unknown force were moving it, commanding him to not abandon the rock he had claimed. "We'll get splinters."

"I get splinters every day. No big deal. Come on."

Olsen dawdled to the cave entrance as slowly as if his foul-smelling Aunt Ebba had gestured for him to come hug her.

"I'll grab this end and you grab that end. "One. Two. Three. Pull."

The board came loose easily enough that Olsen toppled backwards, yelping as he landed in a sitting position on ancient road gravel.

Snook dropped to her knees. "Are you in one piece?"

Olsen stared toward the surrounding woods, worried if someone had seen him fall. Shame would hurt worse than a buttocks slam. "Ain't hurt none." He rolled to one side, groaning as he pushed up from the ground.

Snook brushed dirt off her friend's rump. "Let's yank

off a couple more boards so I can squeeze in."

Once they pried loose more planks, they poked their heads through the gap, startled by damp air exhaling from the hillside's throat.

Olsen coughed and turned his head to the side. "That smells awful."

Snook leaned in farther. "One more board and I can climb in."

Olsen clutched Snook's shoulder. "That smell is gas. Grandmommie won't let me anywhere near her oven cause gas is poison."

Snook shook her head. "Smells like old farts to me. Like Mr. Ricci's hound stinks."

Olsen shook his head and retreated farther. "Hercules's farts can kill people. They make me puke."

"Then stay out here by yourself. See if I care." Snook straddled a board and poked a leg in.

"Don't," Olsen screamed.

"I'll be back before you can count to fifty." Snook slid her upper body forward, pulled her other leg in, and disappeared.

Olsen moved to resting beneath a giant white oak, the lone tree surviving in the battle-scarred clearing where patches of knee high, sickly appearing scrubby vegetation struggled. He laggardly counted aloud as his voice trembled greater with each number.

While swatting at persistent gnats desiring sips of his sweat, he reached fifty and paused. He stared at the entrance to hell and began a second round of counting. When he reached thirty-eight, he stood, stared for a long minute at the cave mouth, approached it, and rubbed his foot back and forth over the keep-out warning splayed on the ground.

He leaned in the cave opening, grimaced at the smell, and yelled Snook's name. His voice echoed as happened every time he yelled down old Mr. Russell's well.

"I'm coming," Snook yelled from back in the cavern.

Olsen sighed, collapsed beside the opening, and whispered to the sky. "Thank you, God."

Snook grabbed onto a board and pulled herself out, coughing several light huffs. "I need to come back with a flashlight or a candle."

She peered down at her friend. "Are you okay? Are you crying?"

3. COMPANY STORE SNITCHING

Eliza Tate climbed Epperly Hill, toting her wicker basket to the company store to purchase canned beans, cornbread mix, rice, onions, flour, eggs, and a few potatoes.

Upon entering, she clamped a perfumed handkerchief to her face, accustomed to Mr. Ricci passing gas and blaming Hercules curled up behind the counter.

Mr. Ricci looked up from polishing apples. "Good morning, Mrs. Tate. Allergies still pestering you?"

Eliza nodded as she always did at Mr. Ricci's immutable question.

Mr. Ricci pointed at a cooler. "We have fresh catfish John Lee Wozniak's boy brung in."

Eliza politely shook her head. "Just my usual, but thank you, Mr. Ricci."

While Eliza shopped, Mr. Ricci retrieved a stack of one-dollar bills from the register and assured George Washington was face up and staring to the right.

As Eliza placed each item on the counter, Mr. Ricci pressed metal keys on his National Cash Register and pulled the crank to enter amounts, ringing the bell. "How is Miss Snook doing? Better I hope."

Eliza frowned, sickened that Mr. Ricci's gas fumes had intensified. "Why would you think Snook ain't well?"

Pulling the crank again, Mr. Ricci peered over his reading glasses. "Miss Bushby was in here. Said Miss Snook missed two days of school."

Eliza placed three onions on the counter and waited for the tally.

Mr. Ricci entered the price of onions one at a time. "She said Snook is her smartest student. That will be three dollars and twelve."

Eliza slid three dollars across the counter. "I must have forgotten my change purse. I'll place one can of beans back on the shelf."

Mr. Ricci puckered his lips and sighed before speaking. "Beans go on special tomorrow. Let's call it three dollars even."

"Thank you, Mr. Ricci."

As Eliza departed the store, Mr. Ricci yelled after her. "Tell Miss Snook I hope she feels better."

Eliza strolled among Epperly Hill houses, passing a family whose house she cleaned. The parents behaved as if Eliza were invisible. Only their four-year-old daughter returned her smile.

Eliza made her way down the hill, wanting to curse out loud—at least curse inside her private thinking—but elected to maintain a calm mind and composure.

When Snook returned from school, Eliza was sitting in the rocker on their front porch. In her lap was a switch she had ripped from their birch tree.

Snook stared at the switch. "What'd I do?"

"You know what you did, Jessie Rae Tate. Don't act innocent."

Snook shrugged.

"You wanna tell me where you were the two days you skipped school?"

Snook shrugged again and mumbled, "Hiking."

Eliza's voice raised an octave. "To that trestle again?"

Snook lowered her head until her chin collided with her chest.

"How many times do I have to forbid you?"

Snook remained still.

"Go cut me a thinner birch branch."

Snook knew thinner branches tear deeper into flesh.

As the switching was executed, Snook prided herself that she had not cried during switching since she was six, an act that angered her mother further.

"Go to your room. Don't be expecting supper tonight."

As Snook crept toward her room, Eliza approached the dining credenza, one of two pieces of furniture she had inherited from her grandmother. She opened the top drawer to return cotton napkins she had folded earlier. But there was a space where something was missing. Was it the serving spoons? No. Those were in the drawer below. The candles were in place as were steak knives that had not been used since the first year she was married. The formal salt and pepper shakers were in their assigned positions, but there was definitely a space in the always-full drawer.

The flashlight. The flashlight was missing. She couldn't remember using it since a thunderstorm in early spring caused all of Winding Gulf to lose power.

She shouted, "Jessie Rae? Do you know where the flashlight is?"

"No Mama."

4. VAPORS

Snook waited until the weekend to return to the cave, tortured since it took Saturday morning forever to arrive.

Olsen frustrated her with his typical weekend nagging to tag along. She feared if she refused him, he would inform his grandmother, and Granny Nielsen was heralded as the biggest gossiper in Raleigh County.

Once again, Olsen aggrieved her by prolonging their hike by a valuable half hour.

Snook reached into her army-green knapsack that her twenty-year-old cousin Lance gifted her after noticing her salivating over it. She retrieved a Baby Ruth chocolate bar and presented it to Olsen. "Savor this while I'm gone. Make it last and I'll give you another when I return."

Olsen appeared as overjoyed as if Snook had bequeathed him her BMX boy's bike—a hand-me-down from cousin Lance's boyhood.

During her initial descent and her first school-day descent into the cave, vapors had made her feel dizzy and nauseated. Although the second school-day descent had made her cough, overall, she had felt more like she was entering a pleasant dream.

On today's fourth descent, again shining her mother's flashlight, everyday colors were enrapturing—colors as bedazzling as July-the-fourth fireworks. Her mood was ecstatic, feeling she possessed power to roll boulders with a simple touch.

Were fumes affecting her? Didn't matter. She relished the disorienting sensations.

She rounded a bend and was allured by a bronze-orange stone slab. She ran her fingers across the unnaturally smooth monolith, sensing electricity flow from the stone into her fingers and course throughout her body. Colors of the rainbow danced behind her eyes. Sweet smells of peeled oranges and neighbors' Hyacinth swathed every molecule of her being. Why would she ever return earthside?

But suddenly she knew. Today, there were messages. Messages from the cave. Messages begging to be delivered to people above going about business as usual, oblivious to the knowing residing in the bedrock.

Although Olsen was relieved to see Snook return topside, he fixated on receiving his second Baby Ruth.

As Snook handed it to him, he was alarmed by her pallor and the change from her usual restlessness to an eerie tranquility. "What's the matter, Snook? You see a ghost?"

Snook sat on the ground with legs crossed as if prepared to meditate. "No ghosts. No angels. No devils."

Olsen stared at a ladybug inching up a weed, thinking there must be more to Snook's story. His Uncle Willie always spun yarns on Halloween of seeing Frederik Tate's ghost floating through the mines. Maybe Snook had seen her father in the cave.

Olsen turned to ask Snook if she saw her father, but when he saw her jaw clamped like a bulldog, he remained silent and ripped off his reward's wrapper.

5. COLD-HEARTED STONE

Hoping additional messages from the cave would speak to her, Snook broke into her yellow ceramic piggy bank and purchased a fresh, unlined notebook and a pack of eight crayons. She would be able to color-code images.

She attempted to sneak past Olsen's house, but he spotted her.

She glared at him. "You got nothing better to do than sit out here all day and spring traps when I pass by?"

"I was reading my comic and you just happened by, smarty pants."

Snook exhaled so much air, she wheezed. "Uh-huh."

"I'll grab my ball hat."

"If you don't never play ball, it ain't a ball hat. It's just a hat."

When they had climbed uphill as few steps as they had fingers and toes, Olsen asked, "Did you bring me a Baby Ruth?"

"Nope."

He halted and pouted. "Why not?"

"Cause I don't owe you. Sides, I don't need you no more."

"I thought you brung me Baby Ruths cause you like me."

"I only like you sometimes. Sides, I can't afford Baby Ruths every time."

Olsen tugged on Snook's elbow. "So, maybe next time?"

"Quit talking or you'll get out of breath faster and slow me down even more."

Snook tried to not feel bad over Olsen's long face, but she did. "Maybe two times from now."

Olsen perked up, but Snook doubted hope and promise would sustain her tagalong much beyond the moment.

Throughout past days and nights, Snook had lounged around home summoning memories of the bronze-orange slab as if it were a new friend. She obsessed about it, yearned to be with it, touch it, have its presence flood her senses.

She crawled through the cavern and arrived at the area with a vaulted ceiling where the monolith lay. It was magnificent as ever, and yet, no message was journeying into her. Although she felt dizzy, felt joy flooding throughout her chest and limbs as before, she was receiving no message.

Her heart missed beats and her breathing became shallow as she worried their relationship had ended. Had she done something wrong? She had lied to her mother about the flashlight. Had been short on patience with Olsen. Had ignored Reverend Charles's sermon in church. Surely that didn't matter. The reverend's lengthy homily was a repeat from last month—not that she had paid attention to earlier renditions. How often must she bear hearing Noah built a boat, or Eve fed Adam, or David sling-shot a giant? And yet, maybe those tiny transgressions had jeopardized her amity with the edifice.

She planted both hands on the smooth stone. "Please come back to me. My heart is set on learning from you."

Nothing happened.

The stone had held promise. But now she sat in the dark, feeling stupid she was being stood up by a rock.

She turned off her flashlight and sat in pure darkness, not wanting the stone or spirits—or bats if there were any—to view her demoralized face.

She began to see small flashes of white lights, the kind of flashes that occur whenever she rubbed her eyes too hard. Surely the flashes were inside her eyes, and yet they appeared to be shimmering out in the universe.

The flashes rocketed into being an artist's full palette

of colors. Was her imagination galloping out of control? Could she reach out and snare the flashes?

The flashes took shape. Not letters. Not symbols she knew. But shapes brimming with meaning.

She wanted to turn on her flashlight, but worried doing so would scare off the flare storm. End the spectacular show that proved she and the amazing gift were locked in a relationship. That was exactly what this stone was. A gift.

Could she remember what she was seeing to sketch in her notebook?

After concentrating deeper while absorbing shapes, she grew confident she could recapture the light show in her notebook. But she would need to do so immediately before memory decayed or became contaminated by scourges and torments of the common world.

She flipped on her flashlight and secured the magic onto her blank pages.

Before departing, she placed her hand on the stone. "I vow to guard these secrets you believe me worthy to receive."

Snook arrived outside, reluctant to swap the cavern for the outside world.

"Golly Snook." Olsen's voice was quivering. "I thought maybe there had been a cave in or a giant snake swallowed you."

"Don't exaggerate, Olsen. I weren't in there long enough for you to pee in the woods and get back."

"No, Snook. I got my Mickey Mouse watch on. You was in there five hours. What was you doing?"

"I wasn't in there even half an hour."

"Look at my watch."

Snook was taken aback. Olsen was correct. Five hours had passed.

6. WAITING IN THE DARK

Snook sat at her mother's dressing table, a piece of furniture passed down three generations on her mother's side. Snook knew nothing of her great-great-grandmother's first or surname, but knew the vanity table and its full-length mirror anchored Eliza to a treasured past.

To one side lay Eliza's gold necklace with a nickel-size, heart-shaped pendant. Snook had never minded that the colors of the pendant and chain did not match. They had been a gift from her father to her mother.

Snook often played with the necklace, swinging and twirling the pendant. She yelled to Eliza across the hallway in the lavatory. "How old were you when Daddy gave you your pendant necklace?"

As she crossed the hallway, Eliza's voice wavered from forcefully towel-drying her hair. "What have I told you other times when you asked?"

"Seventeen."

"Yes ma'am. Still true."

Snook rubbed a finger across the tiny lettering on the pendant: *You hold my heart, Love Frederik.* "Were you married when Daddy gave this to you?"

"Your father proposed a week later."

Snook pondered for a moment. "Was the locket a test to see if you liked it before he asked you to marry him?"

Eliza flapped the towel hard as if expecting that could dry it. "I definitely was hoping he would propose. All weeklong I went overboard complimenting that dainty chain and pendant."

"But did you really like it?"

"It was from your father. That was all that mattered." Eliza leaned near the mirror and stretched her skin to examine a new fissure. "Don't twist the pendant so hard. You'll yank it loose."

Snook set the pendant on the dresser and spiraled the chain around it as her mother did nightly. "How old were you when I was born?"

"Eighteen. Stop doing the math. That's rude."

"I already did the math."

Dressed in her slip, Eliza slipped beneath the covers.

Snook stared at Eliza testing several sleeping positions and finally settling. "Why don't you sleep wearing the necklace if it means so much to you?"

Eliza faced the wall away from Snook. "Well … I like it waiting for me over there on the dressing table. Watching me."

"Guarding you?"

"Perhaps. Watching and guarding."

"But you don't want it closer?"

Eliza huffed, tempted to command Snook to her room—as was required most evenings. But after pondering a moment, she answered. "I like my necklace where it is. I like to know it's there in the dark. That it is waiting for me."

Snook gnawed on a fingernail for a moment. "Like Daddy's waiting there?"

Eliza huffed again, fluffed her pillow, plopped her head on it again, and spoke with a breathy voice. "I suppose in a private way. It's past your bedtime."

Snook remained silent.

Eliza had no doubt what fantasies were dancing in Snook's head, so she addressed them. "One of my favorite moments every night was when I knew your father was standing there in the dark. Knowing he would soon come to me. As much as I adored when he did, there was something special, something electric about feeling him there in the dark, not moving, but trusting he would soon seek me out. The waiting was better than I can describe. Someday you'll have that with someone. Now goodnight."

Snook trudged down the short hallway to her room, thinking, will I really have that someday? And then she thought about Twinkles in her shoebox and Mr. Gammon in his cage, waiting in her room, always excited—or at least pleased—to see her. She froze in place, not wanting to move. She was fairly certain she was feeling what her mother described. The waiting, the knowing who or what would be with her any moment—even if not immediately—was a sweetness warming her head to toe. And at last, giving her goosebumps.

After not hearing Snook's door open and close, Eliza called out, "Snook? Are you going to bed or not?"

"In a minute, Mama. I'm enjoying the waiting before I see Mr. Gammon and Twinkles."

Eliza dragged her second pillow over her head and blocked out night sounds.

7. CRAYON ART

Miss Bushby took a break from averaging student test scores and inched along rows of students answering essay questions about the story she had read in class. Questions ranged from simplified questions for third graders to almost adult questions for fifth graders.

She paused at Snook's desk and glared at crayons scattered on her desk and at a strange image Snook was creating in an unofficial notebook.

Miss Bushby tapped Snook's desk with the end of her curved-tip cane used to hook a slide-projection screen to pull down over the blackboard. The teacher was amazed the girl did not flinch.

Miss Bushby cleared her throat, but still the girl did not respond.

She pressed the end of her cane into Snook's hand, pinning it to her notebook.

Snook looked up as if waking from anesthesia, barely aware of her whereabouts.

Miss Bushby waited until Snook's drifting eyes met her own and whispered, "That is not the assignment."

Snook's focus returned to her notebook, scowling as she slid it aside and retrieved her one-paragraph essay.

Miss Bushby read the paragraph and nodded. "Excellent. Only correction is you misspelled *ingratiating*. Interesting choice for a third grader." She tapped her cane beside the notebook. "What were you drawing?"

Snook shrugged. "Symbols I guess."

"I can see that. What kind of symbols?"

Snook puckered her lips, paused, puffed out air, pursed her lips, shrugged, and stared out the window long enough that Miss Bushby tapped her cane again. "I asked you: what kind of symbols?"

"Oh … I suppose … uh … ideas."

"The symbols represent ideas?"

Snook maintained staring at the school yard. "I guess."

Miss Bushby pulled up a spare chair, sat beside Snook, and glared at the girl staring at nothing. "What sort of ideas?"

"Oh … uh … different things … weather … storms … droughts … different things."

"Are you expressing these ideas … in some sort of a different language?"

"Not exactly language."

"Oh." Miss Bushby sat erect. "How does one express ideas without language?"

Snook locked eyes with her teacher. "Same as paintings … or music … or dance. No words needed."

"The arts?"

"If that's what you want to call them."

"Where did you learn these images? See them?"

Snook shut her eyes. "In my head. Like when I see a dog. And I close my eyes. And I see it again. But changed. And then I draw that."

"Curious." Miss Bushby leaned back in her chair. "Maybe we should ask Miss Goodman if you could participate in her art classes. Could be you are blessed with an aptitude for art."

Snook sat still.

"What do you think?"

Snook crossed her arms on her desk and rested her head on them, muffling her speech. "I like Miss Goodman, but I prefer to draw on my own time."

"Well. You are in school at this moment. And happen to be in my class. This is not your time. This is a time we dedicate ourselves to assignments. To nothing else."

Snook glared at her teacher without speaking.

"Is that clear?"

"Yes ma'am."

Miss Bushby snatched the notebook, returned to her desk, and locked Snook's notebook in her side drawer.

8. SCHOOL CONFERENCE

Eliza Tate had never owned a car and never learned to drive. She asked their neighbor Rosie Hatfield to drive her and Snook to the school.

From the front passenger seat of Rosie's 1953 Ford, Eliza spoke to Snook over her shoulder. "It still don't make no sense why we have to meet with Miss Bushby and Principal Falwell if you ain't in trouble for skipping school them two days."

"I'm not. I already told you."

"Your grades are straight A's."

"I know. I know."

"Then what?"

Snook shrugged.

As soon as Eliza and Snook were seated at a round table with Principal Falwell and Miss Bushby, Falwell slid a notebook across the table. "Your daughter brought this to class."

Eliza glanced at Snook, opened the notebook with caution as if fearing a black widow may spring out, stared at the first page, thumbed through a few pages, closed the notebook, and frowned at the two adults across the table. "I don't understand. What is this?"

Falwell fielded the question. "We aren't certain. *Symbols* your daughter told us. Symbols that tell prophesies—or so she insinuated."

"Prophesies?" Eliza turned to Snook. "Where did you get these?"

Snook shrugged. "I drew them."

Eliza leaned forward with elbows on the table. "She's scribbled ever since she could grasp a pen or a pencil or a crayon. I don't see why this is of concern."

Miss Bushby started to speak but halted when Falwell

placed his hand on her arm. "We shared these works—these symbols—with a professor at Marshall College in Huntington. Professor Rothman studies world cultures. He found that many symbols in your daughter's notebook resemble Norse or Viking symbols. Ancient Germanic cultures. *Runes or glyphs* the professor called them. Various meanings. Protection of ships. Protection of travelers. Over centuries, they were adopted for multiple purposes in Prussia, in Sweden, in Norway. Germany adopted one image as their Nazi swastika."

Snook erupted with disgust. "I have nothing like a swastika in my chronicling."

Falwell leaned back with a startled expression. "Did you say chronicling?"

Miss Bushby piped in. "I use that word in my assignments—have the kids chronicle."

"I see." Falwell turned to Eliza. "My concern—our concern—is that these symbols—although not exacting of the ancient markings—are images with a tainted history."

Falwell slid a book opened to a page for Eliza to review. "This image Professor Rothman called a Hagalaz. It is associated with the underworld."

Snook grimaced. "I ain't never heard that word."

"Do you agree or disagree that this looks like one of the images you drew?"

Snook shut her eyes. "Sort of."

Falwell referred to the book. "The Nazi SS wore that symbol, saying, 'Seeds of the new age are borne through darkness and destruction.'"

Snook rolled her eyes and huffed. "Like winter. It gets dark and cold. Then explodes into spring with new life."

Falwell leaned forward with keener interest. "Did you make up that story like you did the images?"

"Reverend Charles uses that parable in church every

other sermon. You've never heard that, Mr. Falwell?"

Snook grinned as did Eliza, but the principal remained stone-faced.

"And this one." Falwell turned the pages to a second bookmark for the mother and daughter to review as he read aloud. "It represents racially, biologically, hereditarily valuable families of SS members—and other Aryans." He glared at Snook. "Overall, young lady, your drawings appear to be unchristian, unholy."

Snook yelled, "I did not copy anything unholy out of your unholy book or from anywhere."

"So, tell me. Where did these images come from?"

Snook slid her body as far back in her seat as possible and crossed her arms. "They came to me."

Falwell exchanged glances with Miss Bushby. "Came to you from where?"

"Sitting by a rock. Satisfied?"

Again, the educators exchanged glances.

Falwell continued with his face displaying piquing curiosity. "And where might we locate this rock?"

Snook hugged herself tighter. "The rock is special to me. It's nothing I will ever share with you or nobody else."

The three adults exchanged multiple glances as if playing a game of pass-the-hot-potato.

Eliza addressed her daughter with a soft tone. "Jessie Rae Tate? I raised you better than that. Principal Falwell politely asked you a question, honey."

Snook shook her head like a dog shaking off water. "He accused me of being unholy, Mama. That ain't close to being polite. I don't care to tell this man anything more. End of discussion."

She shut down like a wind-up toy that had run down.

After a moment, Miss Bushby spoke. "Mrs. Tate, maybe we could talk with you alone for a moment."

Snook stormed out of the room.

9. FIRE WITH FIRE

Principal Falwell is dead wrong and two can play games, Snook thought. If that creep has people following him into stupidity, I can have people follow me to truth.

But where to begin? Maybe practice on Olsen. But he's only seven. Truth for him is a chocolate bar.

Perhaps cousin Lance can help. But he's twenty. Old enough he's set in his ways. But his girlfriend Trisha is seventeen. Always seems interested in what I have to offer.

She knew Trisha, her parents, and Trisha's twelve-year-old brother lived in one of the foremen houses on Epperly Hill.

The day was early. She could ride her bike to Epperly Hill and still have time to explore ruins of the Collins Temple Baptist Church or scale the Camp Two trestle before racing home.

She stood on the porch of Trisha's house, one of six in a row of foremen family houses. None were as grand as houses purchased by higher ranking foremen who painted their homes with bright colors to prove they had broken free from colliery-debt shackles. But still, these houses were far nicer than typical company homes—or *shacks* as many labeled them.

She hesitated knocking. How do you explain to someone that you climbed into a cave, admired a gold-colored rock, and wisdom was shared with you through images that only you can translate? And that translating such wisdom into human words would be an insult to the ideas?

A yappy pup inside announced her arrival. Maybe she should have approached Lance first.

Trisha's mother answered while dusting her flour-coated hands on her apron. "Can I help you?"

The coldness of her voice signaled Snook that she had interrupted someone who resents being disturbed.

"Hi. I am Jessie Rae Tate from down in Winding Gulf. Lance is my first cousin. I know Trisha through him. Is she home? If not, I can drop by some other time."

The woman yelled over her shoulder, "Trisha? Lance's cousin Jessie Rae is here looking for ya."

A voice from deep inside yelled, "Tell her, I'll be right there."

"She'll be right here. Have a seat on the porch." She closed the door.

Rude, Snook thought. Maybe she's snooty cause me and Lance come from common-worker families. Not highfalutin foremen families. Glad I didn't plan on speaking with that persnickety creature.

She took a seat in one of three non-matching chairs as the pup continued to yap from inside.

The half dozen unpainted two-story row houses were identical, only distinguishable by varying porch furniture or absence of furniture. She wondered why people would not sit on their porches. Coal dust in the air?

Trisha stepped out. "Hi Snook. Didn't expect to ever have a visit from you. Can I get you some water? Iced tea?"

"I just drank water, but thank you."

Trisha sat in the chair beside Snook. "What brings you up Epperly Hill?"

"Strolling. Sometimes I go camp to camp, sometimes climb the Camp Two trestle."

"Oh my gosh. By yourself? You could never get me to even crawl across that rickety thing, much less walk on or climb it. Does your mother know?"

Snook blushed. Telling her mother was not a consideration. Should she lie? "Oh, Mama don't mind—

but don't say nothing."

Trisha's head wobbled between nodding and shaking no, confusing Snook and herself.

Maybe approaching Trisha was a bad idea. She had an urge to flee, but Trisha appeared poised to listen.

Snook leaned forward, talking in a low voice so that neighbors, walls, birds, or any real or imagined gossiping agent could not hear.

She laid the groundwork by telling of Olsen and Baby Ruths and the keep-out sign and the flashlight and the majestic rock.

Now came the difficult hurdle.

"Maybe it was the gas fumes or other vapors in the cave, Trisha. Something in that dank air made me dizzy. And then, I felt the earth talking—not actually talking—but communicating. Images. More than that. Images chocked full of meaning. Stories but not stories. Warnings but not warnings. I could feel, almost taste what was passing into me."

Snook felt she was losing her only audience member. Trisha looked both perplexed and minus of thought, like the time Miss Bushby showed the class what she called, "abstract art." Snook and classmates had stared at a canvas of splashed paint, attracted but unmoved all at once.

Words were failing her. "Wait. Let me show you my glyphs."

"Your what?"

"Glyphs. Images. What a professor called them."

Snook pulled out a batch of folded papers. "I drew these in a notebook, but my teacher stole it and locked it in her desk. Lucky for me, I had made copies on the back of old homework assignments."

She unfolded the papers and Trisha frowned upon first glance. She carefully dragged her index finger down the page, cautious to avoid touching the markings, studying each image as if filing them to memory.

Snook felt relieved that this human sitting beside her was treating her images with devotion, respecting something that Snook treasured. But were the images truly speaking to Trisha? Or were the images provoking her eyes as did *Life Magazine* war photos or postcard lynching photos? Images that churn stomachs and don't offer hope.

Either way, the images from the cavern were waltzing in Snook's mind without words. How could she and Trisha—or anyone—discuss them with words?

Trisha whispered so softly that Snook filled in what she thought she heard. "These are magnetic—or some word I don't know."

Snook's eyes teared. "There are no words." She settled back in her chair. "And yet, now I know things. Things Mother Earth wants me to know. I feel droughts and storms and poison in air and water."

Trisha crossed her arms over her chest as if needing armor. "Why would Earth do that?"

Snook kneeled beside Trisha and whispered into her ear. "I can't feel the why. Least not yet. But people need to know."

Trisha nodded. "It's important you share what you know."

"My teacher and principal and mother don't feel the same. They acted horrified. Not by messages—cause I ain't explained nothing to them. But they acted horrified I drew them images."

Trisha nodded. "There is horror here. And there is also beauty."

"Exactly. Both."

Snook scooted a chair beside Trisha and they studied more pages as Trisha dragged her finger down each row, pausing beside particular images that resonated deeper.

Snook focused on Trisha's face, recognizing vacillating joy and agony.

Once Trisha completed her journey through Snook's cavern paradoxes, she returned the papers. Her eyes and smile were gentle. "Thank you, Snook."

Trisha closed her eyes and settled back in her chair. "What do you plan to do with these?"

Snook also settled back with closed eyes, feeling a need to detach from sunlight and coal dust and distant chugging of coal machinery. "I can't keep this knowing for myself. That would be selfish."

"You should share."

Snook chuckled. It felt good to have someone in the world on her side. And to think she almost had run from the porch.

Trisha shook Snook's arm. "Did you share these with your friend Olsen?"

"Are you kidding? Baby Ruths is all that big-head boy needs to pacify him."

They both laughed, closed their eyes again, and clung to being in content inner worlds, knowing the other was close by.

Snook thought, that's what it's about, isn't it? Discovering and sharing.

But with whom else should she share? There are many people out there deserving to be alerted to truth. But how to go about sharing?

Trisha cleared her throat and yanked Snook from her trance with her excited speech. "I know. Let's talk with Lance. Soon as he returns from Ohio."

Snook pushed forward with her elbows, almost toppling out of her chair. "Lance?"

"He'll have ideas how to help. Always does."

"But Lance is stuck on coalmining and baseball and

tinkering with cars. What if he attacks these images like my teacher and principal done?”

“Calm down, Snook.” Trisha waved her hands gently to signal Snook to settle. “Lance has a thoughtful, quiet intelligence he hides from people.”

Snook sat quietly with a sour look of repugnance as strong as if she had witnessed Trisha’s yappy pup rush into the street and be smashed by a coal truck.

“Really, Snook. We can trust Lance.”

10. COUSINLY COUNTENANCE

Summer break offered freedom to wear blue jeans every day and break free from ignorant adults bossing her.

Snook rode her bike back and forth on Winding Gulf Road while Trisha talked with Lance inside his parents' log-cabin-style home.

Perhaps talking for so long meant Trisha was having difficulty explaining a mystery as fantastical as ancient myths, Biblical stories, and comic-book adventures all braided together.

Snook ambled to a creek bleeding orange from coal-mining activities, and targeted rocks into the water. One splash avenged her above-the-knees white shorts. She would be in big trouble for the quarter-size stain. Even spitting on her hand and rubbing the spot did not help. Maybe Lance or Trisha could wipe her carelessness away.

She returned to Lance's porch, put her ear to the door, and listened to mumbling long enough for shifting sun to thwart porch shade.

Trisha and Lance stepped outside and sat in a wicker loveseat with Trisha holding Lance's hand in her lap. "I explained as best as I could, Snook. Lance has questions." She faced Lance. "Go ahead."

Lance squinted as if thinking deeply about how to phrase his thoughts, relaxed his face, and then squinted again. "Where is your cave?"

"Or old mine?" Trisha added.

Snook sat up straight as if on a witness stand. "Up toward Mitchell Ridge. I discovered the entrance hiking up an over-grown trail."

Lance slid his hand free from Trisha's grip and leaned toward Snook. "You told Trisha the large rock is inside, right?"

Snook appeared skeptical as if a lawyer were trying to trick her. "Big as a school bus. Looks like the ceiling caved in. Bronze color. Smooth."

Lance held a page of Snook's drawings close to his face. "Were these marks drawn on or carved in the stone?"

Snook shook her head.

"But you saw them on the rock?"

Snook stared at her feet. "I felt them."

"I don't understand."

"It's hard to explain." She stared at a mountain top as if it might whisper an answer. "Picture you are looking in a little brook. You drop in a stone and ripples blur the bottom. Then the water calms. You begin to make out pebbles and sand grains. Not good at first, but then clear as can be. Something sloshes the water. Again, you can't make out what's there. But now it's different. You remember what you saw even clearer in your head."

Snook buried her head in her crossed arms. "You don't believe me, do you?"

Lance waited a moment. "Look at me, kid."

Snook took in several deep breaths before looking.

"Just cause I don't understand, don't mean I don't believe you." Lance moved to sitting beside Snook and put his arm around her back. "When you were two, barely high as my knee, you were my little tough-as-a-soldier gal. You still are."

Snook collapsed her head on her cousin's lap. "What am I gonna do, Lance?"

Lance patted Snook's shoulder. "Trisha says you feel there's no way you can push aside what you saw—felt."

Snook mumbled from Lance's lap. "People gotta know."

"You always have wanted what's good for other folk. A reason you're my champ."

Snook sat up. "So, you can help me?"

"Not sure where to start. But me and you and Trisha'll

put our heads together. Figure something out."

"People will think we're stupid—or plum crazy."

"People always think something's stupid or crazy when that something's new or powerful. We can't make people think different than they're built. All we can do is lay truth at their feet and give them time. What they do is up to them."

"Like see if fish will take the bait?"

Lance chuckled so hard he choked and had to cough a moment. "When fish take the bait, they end up fried and eaten. We're hoping people will change. Grow. Live better. Right kid?"

Snook hugged her cousin tighter. She didn't say it, but thought it. Lance was some kind of cross between a big brother and a father. More than ever, she needed him to keep being that.

11. BANDANA

As soon as Snook woke, she sprinkled bits of catfish and chicken onto cornmeal she had soaked overnight. She placed the mixture on the porch and released Mr. Gammon from his cage. He sniffed a multitude of times and then glared at Snook as if suffering insult.

"Sorry, Mr. Gammon. We barely have any fish left."

Mr. Gammon shoved food around with his nose until it was arranged perfectly to satisfy his demand for order.

Trisha arrived moments later and joined Snook on the porch.

Snook scanned the landscape. "I thought Lance was coming with you."

"He'll be here momentarily. He was up late last night with his pals discussing your situation."

Snook's posture shifted to full alert. "He didn't tell them about my drawings, did he?"

"You agreed he could last night."

"Not right away. We agreed we'd sleep on it. Why did he jump the gun? Who did he tell?"

"Guys from his baseball team."

"Like who?"

"Friends he trusts."

"How many?"

"I don't know, Snook. Henry Yates. Johnny Banbury. A couple others."

"Holy crap."

"Don't curse. You agreed to this plan last night."

"Not a truck load of people."

"There were only four—five at most."

"They'll tell others. And then they'll tell their families and friends." She shut her eyes. "This was a big mistake."

"Lance swore them to silence."

Snook collapsed into a slouched position in a rocker and tucked her feet up onto the seat, compacting her size like a turtle in retreat. "Good luck with his drinking buddies keeping their mouths shut."

"Look at me, Snook." Trisha kneeled so their faces were even. "You asked for help to spread the word about your remarkable experience."

Snook buried her face into her knees.

Trisha used an even gentler tone. "Lance wants to show them an image or two."

Snook slammed her head against the rocker's back and stared at the porch ceiling.

Trisha backed away. "It's difficult to convince people if you don't offer some kind of proof. Lance needs two of your drawings."

"Principal Falwell seen my drawings. That got me suspended."

"You didn't have me and Lance and his buddies by your side. You're not alone this time."

Snook hissed like a tire going flat. "Okay. Two. Two drawings. No more."

"Two is a start."

"I can't believe I'm agreeing to this."

"Oh yeah. And one more thing. Lance wants to see the cave."

Snook's eyes widened as round as coffee saucers as she screamed, "No."

"Calm down, Snook. Take a deep breath and think about it. If I came to you with such a story—"

"It's not a story. It's a fact."

"Okay. With such a fact. But if I had no evidence, what would you think?"

Snook thought for a long moment and mumbled as if words were being pulled from her mouth, painful as tooth extractions. "Fine. I'll take Lance there. But blindfolded.

Nobody else."

Trisha had always sensed Snook was much older and wiser than her actual age, but this demand felt no better than an eight-year-old's initiation rite for a club of other eight-year-olds. "Really Snook? Blindfolded?"

"That or nothing."

Trisha paced back and forth on the porch, sat on the loveseat, and stared at a blank area of sky. "I think if me and you gang up on Lance, he might could go along with your blindfold idea. Maybe."

"When?"

"He wants to see the cave before he shares your drawings with his gang."

"So? Tomorrow?"

Trisha remained stone-faced.

Snook suddenly had a look of terror. "You mean today?"

"He's waiting by the creek."

Snook stood on her tiptoes and scoured the creek bank. Sure enough, Lance was sitting on a boulder cooling his bare feet in a waist-high chute. He waved at her.

Trisha rested her hand on Snook's shoulder. "So? Do we have an agreeable plan?"

"I'll grab my bandana. But only Lance can go with me. Not even you."

12. CAVE SMELLS

What had seemed like a good idea—blindfolding Lance—proved to be exasperating.

Snook grabbed Lance's waist. "Stop. You gotta step over another log. About knee high."

Lance slid one foot forward, bumped the log, bent over, sized it with his hands, and straddled over it.

Snook huffed out air. "This is gonna take all day—maybe all week."

"So? What do you want to do?"

"If I let you remove the blindfold, can you promise to not tell nobody where we went?"

"I already have no clue where we are. We waded three brooks. Climbed over a dozen logs. Ducked beneath two trees leaning across the trail. We could be anywhere on this ridge."

"Okay, okay. Pull it off." Snook watched Lance remove the bandana. "Sorry I had such a dumb idea."

"You were protecting something you treasure. That's not dumb. Just difficult to execute." Lance grinned. "I didn't realize you still had the backpack I gave you. You put some mileage on it, kid. Right near worn out."

"Don't matter. It was from you."

Lance scanned the terrain. "You sure this is the way?"

"I sneaked away and hiked this ridge since I was four. I never get lost."

Lance jerked his head. "Four?" He chuckled. "You are one unusual human, Jessica Tate."

Snook lost sense of where she was. No one had called her *Jessica* since she was two. A memory rushed at her of a man bouncing her as she rode his moving leg like it was a pony. Had that been her father? One of her mom's boyfriends?

"You okay, Snook?"

"Uh … yeah. Sure." She survyed the landscape. "Up this way I think."

"You think?"

Snook regained her determined voice. "This way."

Lance followed the girl scrambling up a grown-over drainage ditch, having to tear free of branches coated with briars attacking every few feet. That coupled with humidity drawing sweat and battalions of gnats and mosquitos dive-bombing them, resulted in misery.

Lance paused to stand erect, annoyed from bending over for minutes at a time to deal with low-hanging brush.

Snook slapped her bug-attacked ear. "We're about half way."

After thirty minutes, Snook halted. "Okay. We're close. I'll lead you the last bit. Put your bandana back on."

Lance whined like a three-year-old told to wait in the car. "Really?"

After ten minutes of being led by his hand, and a multitude of zigzags, Lance groaned when Snook made him get on his knees and crawl into darkness that was evident even through the bandana. "Oh my God. This smells awful."

"You can pull the bandana off now." Snook flicked on her flashlight. "This way."

They crawled on hands and knees over patches of dry dust and through patches of mud as Lance coughed from the fumes.

Snook shined her light on the rock. "It's high enough you can stand in this part."

Lance's mouth was agape. The monolith far exceeded the size he had envisioned from Snook's details of her underground adventures.

Snook savored Lance's amazed face. "I told you."

Lance experienced a prolonged coughing spell. "How do

you tolerate this poison air? Don't you feel sick?"

"A little dizzy. I was bad sick the first time. You get used to it."

"I won't." Lance crawled behind a small boulder and vomited several bouts.

Still gagging, he returned to Snook. "I can't stay in here. I gotta get fresh air."

As they crawled, Lance pleaded, "I can't wear that bandana again. I'll get even sicker."

"You're too sick to remember where we are anyhow."

They slithered into sunlight and fresh air.

Lance collapsed onto his back, staring at blue sky. "Thank God." After several intentionally deep breaths to cleanse his lungs, he mumbled, "That place is dangerous." He turned and assessed Snook. "How is that possible that you look fine?"

Snook shrugged. She looked around at the forest, enjoying the beauty of the gifts the surface offered, and fell into a daze.

After several moments of tending to his own body by deliberately coughing, spitting, blowing nostrils clear, and wiping eyes, Lance noticed Snook's state. "Hey? Are you okay?"

He freaked out when Snook's eyes roll upward with only the whites showing. He grabbed Snook and shook her. "Snook. Snook."

Snook's eyes returned to normal. She smiled toward Lance. "What?"

"Are you okay?"

"I'm fine. Why?"

Lance huffed out air from relief and sat back. "You looked like you turned into a zombie or was dying."

"I'm fine."

"What happened to you just then?"

Snook shut her eyes to be able to recall what she had

experienced. "More images come to me. Beautiful images. Ugly images. Images of hope. Images of destruction. So much, Lance. It come rushing at me. But I remember it all. I gotta grab my notebook out of my backpack and draw the images before I forget."

Lance sat up and stared at his companion a moment, up at the sky, then at the lone giant yellow oak stretching toward the sky.

He did not say, but thought, I'm not sure what happened, but I believe our lives are on a course beyond what I can fathom.

Snook stood—something Lance still felt too shaky to accomplish. She walked to the tree and planted both hands on the trunk. "I want to build something here. A treehouse. In the arms of this mighty oak. I'll use planks I tore off the entrance. Use loose timbers from just inside. A treehouse to mark how special this place is."

Lance flopped onto his back, continuing to feel too weak to stand or walk. Too weak to bother pondering what was happening.

He was soon napping.

13. TREE TEMPLE

Even before roosters crowed, Snook was on her porch waiting for a glimmer of daylight. She had stuffed her backpack with a hammer, a screwdriver, nails, screws, and rope. Everything she needed for construction.

Trisha and Lance would probably search for her, but she ached for a break from being told what she should and should not do.

She felt certain she could manage lifting planks up into the tree. Timbers were another matter. Maybe she could bind them with ropes, toss the ropes over tree limbs, and hoist them. But timbers probably outweighed her. Should she fess up and ask Lance for help? But who in her right mind asks a twenty-year-old guy to build a treehouse?

Her masterpiece would be more than a treehouse. It would be a tree temple. In school, Miss Bushby had told of Greek temples being places of wisdom, temples built atop craters where earth spewed fumes. "Fires of sulfur. Fires of brimstone," she had taught.

Snook felt honored. Mother Earth had chosen her to discover a shaft burrowed into earth and spewing vapors. Chosen her to receive wisdom.

This had to be a tree temple.

After trying to pull two planks up into the tree and failing, she resolved this was not an eight-year-old girl's feat.

Should she admit to Lance she tried and failed? How would she explain to him why she was building a temple in a tree?

She sat on Lance's porch and waited for him to emerge. He immediately noticed a bandage around her thumb and another on her elbow. "Tried to do it by yourself, did you?"

"Try what by myself?"

"Uh-huh." Lance sat in a rocker, sipped coffee, and stretched his legs. "All you have to do is ask. Or is that too difficult for an individual burdened with oodles of pride?"

Snook protracted time as if she had all day to address his inquiry. "Maybe you might could help me."

"Say please."

Snook bit her lip until it bled before conceding. "Please."

"I already laid out a saw and my tool belt and ropes and pullies."

"Pullies?"

"I may be stronger than you, but I know my limits. I could never hoist large timbers without pullies."

Snook wrinkled her nose as she attempted to picture the full task at hand. "It's got to be really sturdy."

Snook had not sketched plans, but pictured her temple vividly enough that she was certain planks and timbers would align perfectly.

Four days later, there was a floor wide enough for three people to stretch out comfortably and walls with gaps for windows and a door. They ran out of materials before being able to install a full roof.

Snook lay on her back staring up at partial ceiling and partial sky. "There are more pieces of wood deeper in the cave."

Lance huffed. "No way I'm worming back in there. That cave tried to kill me. You should keep out of there."

"Uh-huh."

"That was not a convincing answer."

"Lance?"

"Yeah?"

"Did you mind helping me build this?"

For a moment, Lance traveled back in time. "I never got to build a treehouse as a kid. Thanks for inviting me to be a kid for a day—four days."

Snook sucked in a comforting deep breath. "This is more than being two kids, huh?"

"I don't know what this is. Like much of life, we'll see where it goes. Good or bad. Interesting or uninteresting."

"I think it's more than interesting."

"Maybe. You're calling this clubhouse a temple, right?"

"That's what it is."

"Because?"

"Cause ... it's a place of wisdom. Mother Earth's wisdom."

"Wow. That's pretty heavy."

"Truth is heavy."

"I spect so, Snook. I spect so." Lance glanced at his watch. "People are probably wondering where we disappeared to four days in a row—I know my foreman will."

Snook examined her hands. "I have blisters. Do you?"

"My body's accustomed to showing off what kind of jobs I do. Doubt anyone will guess what my job was this week."

Lance paused to enjoy sounds of wind coursing through forest. "What wisdom is now being delivered to your unfinished temple, Jessie Rae Tate?"

Snook sat up, pulled out her notebook. "These."

Lance glanced at a page with a dozen images. "Look chocked full of wisdom to me." He focused on an image. "What's this one mean?"

Snook reviewed the image intensely as if cramming information from a book chapter to summarize for a class presentation—or to an auditorium of standing-room only.

She spoke as if reading from a book. "This one means the earth's gonna flood, not by sweeping torrents, but a drop at a time. And waters seeping up out of land. Seas creeping higher as slow as hair grows. Skies unleashing drops of rain teaspoons at a time until everything is drowning."

"Crap." Lance frowned at the image. "And you get all of that scary stuff out of this one tiny little figure?"

Snook nodded.

"Can you do the same with these other figures? Like this one. Makes me think of sun. Heat."

Snook returned the notebook to her backpack. "We should head home."

14. COAL MINER CONGREGATION

Malcolm Cline, Henry Yates, Johnny Banbury, and Teddy Krakow passed around a bottle of Johnny's grandfather's moonshine. They sipped the strong, neutral-tasting spirit while listening to Lance's account of accompanying Snook in the old Mitchell Mine.

The men did not say so, but Lance's story-telling talent incited the four men to recall seventh-grade when they dared their classmate Allen Fox to climb into that same mine, a shaft where he breathed toxic fumes and died.

Lance blew out air, feeling thankful he had survived his recent underground quest. "Fumes must be milder now. Still noxious enough I got a whopper of a headache and puked my guts out. Snook appeared hardly affected."

Johnny searched others' faces as if seeking permission to speak. "Did you warn Snook about what happened to Allen Fox?"

Lance bit his lip. "I never let on I'd been to the old mine. Acted like I'd never heard of it."

Johnny grimaced. "That ain't right."

Lance sneered. "She already had climbed in there three times. Why ruin a kid's adventure? She was excited. She believed she discovered that place."

Henry cackled. "When I took my family to Ocean City, my youngest boy thought he discovered the Atlantic Ocean. Named it Lake Samuel after hisself."

Everyone chuckled except Malcolm who refused to partake of the group's jovial mood. "You called us here, promising we'd hear about Snook unearthing some mind-blowing thing inside. I'm waiting."

Lance waited for chuckling and fidgeting to dwindle. "Snook found a rock. Big as a school bus was the way she described it. And it is. A giant slab of collapsed ceiling."

Malcolm's drumming fingers revealed his impatience. "And? That's all you got?"

Lance planted his foot on a chair, leaning on his leg as a pulpit. "What's special is what's difficult to wrap my mind around. Don't make fun of me, but that rock communicates with Snook."

Malcolm's eyes widened and he spit into his chew cup. "Are you asking us to believe a rock talks to Snook?"

"Not talking. It creates images. I brought two of her drawings with me." Lance handed over the two pages.

The men turned the pages sideways, upside down, and after settling on what they deemed to be the proper orientation, frowned, and studied the figures in silence.

Teddy spoke first. "Never seen nothing like this fore. Is it some kind of Egyptian writing? Alien writing?"

Malcolm tossed one of the pages onto the table. "I'll tell you exactly what it is. This is the Devil's handicraft. Witchcraft. Unsaintly icons."

Teddy turned his head away to block the group from hearing his murmured profanity.

Johnny picked up the discarded page. "In fifth grade, we had a club. Remember Henry? Me and you made up a secret-code alphabet. Sort of like these."

Henry reached for the page. "These ain't animals or buildings. More like crazy letters or numbers or directions."

Lance sat and tipped his chair back onto two legs. "Snook says these aren't any of those things. They're wisdom. Knowledge of times to come."

"In secret code?" Henry scratched his forehead. "In the Navy, we had signal lights. Flashed Morse code that stood for letters. Spelled out words."

Malcolm crossed his arms as if challenging Lance. "Exactly what kind of knowledge does your eight-year-old little girl cousin say are in these wisdom figures?"

"Yeah," Johnny asked. "What wisdom?"

Lance leaned forward, causing his chair's front legs to slam down onto the floor. "Knowledge that Mother Earth communicates with her. Warnings of things to come."

The group sat in silence.

Malcolm walked to the window, peered out, and circled the room. "Warnings from deep underground. Well, there you have it, fellas. A cave. An entrance to the underworld. Like I said a minute ago, these things are the Devil's handiwork."

Teddy stood with chest out. "Bullshit, Malcolm. Snook's a little girl."

Malcolm glared at Teddy and jabbed his finger at the air as if striking Teddy's chest. "Possessed."

Henry held up his hand, signaling to keep it peaceful. "Let's don't none of us go making a fuss before we know more about this rock."

Malcolm marched to the door and clutched the handle. "I don't need to know more. It's clear. If you four can't see it, then I feel sorry for you."

Malcolm fled the gathering without farewell words or gestures.

15. SKINNED SQUIRRELS

Snook stopped to watch the Collins High School Pirates practice football before sauntering along Epperly Hill. She spotted her classmate, Doris Gravely, walking with her mother. Doris's mother yanked her daughter back, whispered into her ear, and hurriedly towed Doris away.

People on Epperly Hill were often snobbish, but had never behaved as if Snook were a Halloween ghoul rising from the cemetery—or contagious with chickenpox.

Snook continued forward and saw another parent appear alarmed, clutch her child's hand, drag him to the other side of the street, and continue onward as if avoiding a rabid dog.

Snook pounded on Olsen's front door until he arrived, still arranging his glasses on his overly large head and yawning as if waking from a nap.

Snook yelled, "What have you been telling people about me?"

"I don't never say nothing bout you cept you dragged me into the woods."

"Dragged you into the woods? Gosh almighty. That makes it sound like I kidnapped you."

"What's kidnap?"

"Oh my golly, Olsen. I should kidnap you and get you off your behind so you can learn more about this planet."

"I know about this planet."

"Okay. Which way is west?"

Olsen stared four different directions.

Snook slapped her forehead. "Hint. Look at the sun."

Olsen squinted enough that Snook was certain he had completely shut his eyes.

He pointed up. "That way?"

"Oh my golly. That's not west. That's up."

"Are you going to kidnap me?"

From across the street, a woman pointed out Snook to another woman. The two women shook their heads, covered their mouths while whispering, and strutted away, glancing back several times.

Snook yelled, "What in tarnation? Something about me's spooking everybody awful, Olsen. I'm being treated like I have leprosy."

"What's leprosy?"

"A disease where your skin falls off."

Picturing a squirrel his uncle had skinned in front of him, Olsen shuddered.

Snook talked over her shoulder as she marched away. "I'll go meet Lance getting off his shift. See if he knows what's going on."

Lance emerged from Number Two, and as usual was coated in black dust with only the whites of his eyes announcing a person existed beneath. "Hi kid."

"Something's bad wrong, Lance."

Lance sounded alarmed, but his face was too covered in coal dust for emotions to be recognized. "Are you injured? Sick? Somebody die?"

"Everybody's acting like I smell bad or am waving a loaded pistol. Some crossed the road to avoid me. I ain't done nothing, Lance."

Lance sat on a workbench and patted for Snook to sit beside him.

Snook collapsed against him and began crying, an act Lance could not remember witnessing since she had been toilet trained—except for the time she had an abscessed tooth.

Snook remained leaning against Lance, blubbering what almost sounded like words.

"You ain't done nothing bad, Snook. But I got an idea who did and soon as I bath, I'll check it out and get back to you.”

Snook moaned a sound resembling *uh-huh.*

“In the meantime, you stay put, hear? That's an order.”

Snook nodded agreement. As she watched Lance walk away, she futilely attempted to wipe Lance's coal dust from her cheek.

16. WEDNESDAY NIGHT SERVICE

Lance hurried home, tossed his workwear into a tub of water, added distilled white vinegar and baking soda, and cleaned his hands with pumice soap and a scrub brush.

He headed to a Number-One-Camp area where Malcolm Cline and a half-dozen houses of Malcolm's relatives lived; a small section referred to as *Cline Town.*

He spotted an elderly woman in a rocker with skin as gray as if she had been mummified for a thousand years. Lance approached and nodded a greeting. "Good evening. I am looking for Malcolm Cline."

Although the woman's chair was moving as little as if a light breeze were swaying it, she halted rocking. "Malcolm's in church." She nodded toward a nearby structure. "Wednesday evening service."

"Yes ma'am. Thank you."

The matron of the porch resumed her barely detectable rocking. "Should be dismissing right soon."

"Mind if I wait here and look for him?"

"Do what you will. Everyone does these days."

Lance assumed further conversing would be as painful as plucking nose hairs. "I'll take a seat on your stoop."

"Suit yourself."

After a few minutes that felt like hours, people emptied out from a former foreman's house that had been procured as a temporary church.

Malcolm was walking and conferring with a man wearing a baby-blue suit jacket. By his likeness, Lance assessed the man could easily be Malcolm's brother or at least a closely related cousin.

Malcolm appeared startled when he saw his rival baseball team's first baseman. "Holy cow, Lance. Never knowed you to poke your face into Number One Camp. I see you met Granny Austin, my mamaw's sister."

"We did meet, thank you."

Malcolm placed his hand on the other man's shoulder. "Lance? This here is Pastor Lawrence Ezekiel Brown. He relocated from Coal City a few months back."

"Just call me Pastor Ezekiel." The pastor extended his hand. "A pleasure to meet you, brother."

Lance shook hands, feeling abashed after being addressed as *brother.* "Nice to meet you. Welcome Pastor."

Malcolm gestured for Lance to join them proceeding along the unpaved street. "Linda prepared a cake for tonight's gathering. Saved some back at the house. Join us."

"Thank you, Malcolm. I'll take you up on that."

Malcolm winked toward Ezekiel. "This is the co-worker I told you about. The one with the young girl cousin."

"Ah." Ezekiel squinted his eyes and puckered his lips a moment as he seemed to be weighing how to respond. "Very interesting story, I must say. Are you the young fella who showed the girl's images to Malcolm?"

Lance appeared taken aback. "Two images. Yes."

Ezekiel simpered. "I understand your girl cousin is overflowing with prophesies."

Lance thought he should tread lightly as he had learned to do anytime religion or politics rose its head as a topic within coal camps. "I do not consider my cousin Snook's words to be prophesies. So, she certainly cannot be overflowing with prophesies."

"Your little cousin's name is *Snook?*"

"Her proper name is *Jessica. Snook* is a nickname."

"I see." Ezekiel glanced toward his companion with raised eyebrows, and then spoke while staring toward the horizon. "Malcolm described your cousin's vivid beliefs. Her explanations resemble dark prophesies. Akin to spells."

Lance had second thoughts about the cake invitation. "Any chance my cousin was a topic of discussion in church this evening?"

Malcolm sounded overly pleased enough that his words took on the character of rapid boasting. "We most certainly did. During tonight's prayer meeting. Also, this past Sabbath. And in porch conversations. Folks everywhere are fascinated."

Lance halted, forcing Ezekiel and Malcolm to stop and rotate to face him.

Lance stuffed his hands into his pockets and took a step backwards. "Actually, I need to take a raincheck on your cake offer. My sister invited my parents, me, my brother—my actual brother—for dinner. It would be inconsiderate for me to keep my family waiting."

17. HOLLOW RUMBLINGS

Lance called off from work and was squatting on Eliza and Snook's stoop long before the paperboy pitched rolled-up newspapers onto porches of the handful of homes affording such an indulgence.

Eliza spotted Lance outside. "How long have you been waiting out here?"

Lance checked his grandfather's Hamilton Railroad pocket watch, always sensing Pappy smiling when he did. "Thirty minutes or so."

Eliza tightened her housecoat's belt. "I am guessing you have some sane reason."

"I don't know about *sane*." Lance moved to the porch. "The makeshift church in Number One Camp believes— led by Malcolm Cline—Snook's drawings reek of witchcraft."

"Oh my God." Eliza stared a long moment at where the sun hinted it was about to rise. "I expect nothing good outta that Cline clan. They drove many a good family from this hollow."

"That they did." Lance lit a cigarette and quickly checked in with Eliza. "Do you mind?"

"Cigarette smoke mixing with coal dust? It's your body. Although any woman with sense loathes kissing a man who tastes like a chimney."

Lance sucked in and then exhaled the heated vapor. "I used to think Snook took after Frederik, but over the years, it's clear she takes after you."

"God help her."

They heard Snook inside talking. "Morning Mr. Twinkles."

Lance frowned puzzlement. "Twinkles? I thought her cat's name was Mr. Gammon. Did she adopt another stray?"

"Twinkles is her pet field mouse. At least that rodent's boxed up and not gnawing my linens. If it ever breaks loose, Mr. Gammon and all the neighborhood cats are lying in wait."

"Should we tell her about Number One Camp?"

Eliza rolled her eyes. "Tell a child that a clan has it in for her?" Eliza watched the paperboy launch news onto a porch. "How serious is the situation?"

"The Clines recruited a pastor from Coal City."

Eliza smacked a mosquito on her forearm and flicked its squished remains into the yard. "I heard about that fraud. Ladies was gossiping in the company store. They run him off from Coal City. Had a thing for married women of his congregation. Did you meet him?"

"Baby-blue jacket and matching baby-blue socks."

Eliza pressed her cuticles back one by one. "Ever since our ugly meeting with Principal Falwell, I've been holding my breath for the other shoe to drop."

Lance exhaled smoke hard enough it spiraled to the road's edge. "That shoe already dropped."

Snook shuffled out to the porch in fuzzy bedroom shoes, carrying Twinkles in her cupped hands. "You two look glum."

Lance snuffed out his cigarette on the porch railing. "Your suspicions was on target. People are upset. Upset by your drawings."

Snook sat in silence on the porch floor, dangling her feet from a section missing railing.

The three porch dwellers watched the sun rise, enjoying the promise of a new day commandeering the skies, aware of darkness clinging in the landscape's deep folds.

Eliza moved to the threshold. "I'll heat up coffee. Start breakfast. Join us." She disappeared inside.

After kissing Twinkles's furry head and rubbing her against her cheek, Snook turned to Lance. "So, that's why people are giving me dirty looks? My drawings?"

"I spect so."

Lance offered Snook his hand, lifted her up, and led her inside where he eyed the room as if it were his first visit. "What's that old thing in the corner?"

Snook stretched out on the floor, playing catch-and-release with Twinkles. "An ole double cupboard. Mama said Daddy used it for storing logs for the wood stove. We use it for coats and raincoats. Boots and shoes."

Lance examined the cupboard's inside. "Big enough for a person."

Snook rolled over and set Twinkles on her chest. "Am I in danger?"

Lance's entire body twitched. "*Danger* is a strong word."

"Am I?"

Lance thought about fifty Winding Gulf miners losing their lives mining. About the coal wars with ten-thousand-armed coal miners confronting three-thousand lawmen. About the local Ku Klux Klan lynching two black miners.

He shut the cupboard door. "In this chunk of the world, living with danger is our way of life."

18. GAME-TIME LUNACY

Lance was not surprised by the mischief of Cline Town. People there had a reputation for explosive combustion as far back as the mine wars of 1912.

He was, however, surprised by the mischief of his friends Henry Yates and Johnny Banbury. They had also enlisted a transplant pastor for the Number Two Camp: Pastor Horace Flackman from up the road in Sophia.

With fear making Lance sweat and his voice quiver, he dared to ask his friends, "What does your Pastor Flackman say about Snook?"

Johnny grinned ear to ear while Henry began preaching. "Pastor Flackman claims Snook is a prophet like when Moses received the Word of God on Mount Sinai. That she experiences God's voice like God commanding Abraham, Samuel, Elijah, John the Baptist, and all them ancient holy fellas."

Johnny stepped closer to Lance, tapped his shoulder, and spoke with a low voice. "Pastor Flackman is eager to visit the cave. Determined we protect it. Claims that place is sacred ground. Holy soil."

Lance sat, buried his face in his hands, and mumbled, "Snook built a tree temple there."

Both enthusiastic men moved closer to Lance. "Couldn't hear you. What'd you say?"

"Nothing."

Lance was uncertain why his thinking descended into recalling Collins High School students playing Coal City High School students in football every fall. Local fans always went all out, behaving as if the existence of the world depended upon that one event. Throngs holding parades, partying, betting, praying, screaming threats, firing shots into the air, getting intoxicated, racing cars, and concocting a multitude of risk-taking shenanigans.

In her own peculiar way, Snook had lit a fuse sparking its way toward a stockpile of black powder larger than did football games. Mankind was descending into lunacy.

Instead of Collins verses Coal City high schools, it was Number-One-Camp's transplant pastor verses Number-Two-Camp's transplant pastor.

Ezekiel verses Flackman.

19. PACKING-CRATE PREACHING

Days later, when Lance arrived at Number Two Camp mine, he was startled to find the two imported pastors standing on wooden packing crates, each preaching to their own semi-circle of workers.

Standing on the ground beside each pastor were muscular miners with arms crossed and glaring at the crowd. Bodyguards anticipating another mine war? They certainly weren't altar boys.

As he stood midway between the pastors, Lance concentrated enough to distinguish what one at a time was yelling.

Pastor Flackman was sermonizing with a haughty voice, naming Biblical prophets and saints of old, describing ways God addressed each. Burning bush for Moses. Saint Michael for Joan of Arc. Direct conversations with Abraham.

Pastor Ezekiel was screaming with a hoarse voice, naming dark moments of history's witch trials, burnings at the stake, drownings by dunking, and feeding Christians to lions. While shaking his fists for emphasis, he screamed, "False prophets walk among us."

Time to time, a coal miner or two stumbled upon the scene, ambled back and forth between the two assemblies, waved good riddance to the pandemonium, and headed home.

Ezekiel's congregation gasped and cheered louder than Flackman's. Although the sun had yet to set, Ezekiel's followers were waving flaming torches.

The usual custom at the conclusion of mining shifts was for an assortment of women to gather and assure husbands or lovers had returned to the surface alive and unscathed. But this evening, there was an absence of women. Had they been sent away? Scared off?

Lance moved closer to better hear Ezekiel.

"We in this valley are God's tribe. Shall we surrender our souls to the devil by being led astray by false prophets? Led by those who worship images of the beast? Revelations informs us, false prophets were to be thrown into lakes of fire and brimstone."

The crowd cheered with vitriolic shouting, "Lakes of brimstone. Lakes of brimstone."

Lance backed away, constraining his movements, hoping to remain unnoticed.

As he maneuvered past Flackman's group, he eavesdropped. "What is Mother Earth if not the creation of God? She speaks for Him. In our hearts we know Mother Earth's truth is God's truth. Are we to turn a blind eye? Jam our fingers in our ears?"

Flackman's crowd cheered, "No."

"Are we to resist wisdom? Ignore the beauty God bestowed upon us with His gift of earth? Earth. That wondrous source that sustains all life."

Flackman pointed his finger at individuals one after another. "We are called upon to open our senses. Open our hearts. Honor this prophet who walks amongst us."

He stared upward and opened his hands as if grasping the heavens. "When we welcome the truth of Mother Earth, we behold the face of God."

Flackman's crowd cheered as loudly as the other camp's, but with a joyful fervor.

Lance slipped into the darkness and headed toward Trisha's, concerned he may have a target on his back from one group and dangerous adoration from the other.

20. MUSKET

It was early evening when Eliza heard banging on her door as if someone were panicked about a street accident, a nearby house burning, or a mine disaster. She spotted Snook snooping behind her and pointed for her to hide as Lance had instructed.

When Eliza cracked open the door to peek out, Malcolm Cline shoved the door, striking Eliza in the face.

Malcolm stormed inside. "Is the girl here?"

Eliza screamed at him. "Malcolm Cline. You have no right breaking into my house with violence and your bossy, threatening attitude."

Malcolm kicked over a foot stool. "I asked you a question. Is the girl here?"

"Look at you. You're a disgrace busting in here like a common criminal."

Malcolm grabbed Eliza by her hair, slung her to the floor, and motioned for his accomplices to enter.

As the men searched, Eliza pulled herself up, brushed off her dress, and limped to the kitchen broom closet.

A man from a bedroom yelled, "Nobody in here."

Malcolm yelled, "Check the yard out back." He swiveled to face Eliza, finding himself staring at a firearm aimed at his eyes. "Shit."

Eliza spoke through clenched teeth. "You and your trashy crew get your asses off my property. You have to five before I blow your head off. One ... two ..."

Malcolm squinted at the firearm. "What the hell is that? A musket? From where? Fighting Injuns and Brits?"

"Yes. You have a musket aimed at you, you son of a bitch. And yes, it's in working condition."

Holding up his hands in a surrender position and then shifting to signaling *take it easy*, he stepped toward Eliza.

"Not another step, Cline boy."

Malcolm's cringing revealed he detested his nickname left over from sixth-grade goading. "No way that antique can spit, much less blast a musket ball an inch or two."

"This *antique* worked fine the last time I fired it. Want me to prove it?"

Malcolm became aware his gang had returned and were watching.

Pete Daniels snickered. "Looks like Miss Tate's well prepared for Injun attacks, boss. You ain't no redskin, but I bet her musket can snuff you out just fine."

Malcolm shrugged. "I ain't worried. That piece of crap ain't been fired in a hundred years."

Eliza lowered the barrel and aimed at Malcolm's groin. "It fired fine last week when I shot a mouse nibbling on my Geraniums. Mouse was a small little target the size of what I'm sighting my rifle on this minute."

One of the men exploded with laughter. "She's gonna blow your balls off, Cline boy."

Malcolm screamed, "Y'all do something."

Malcolm's brother spoke in a calm tone. "The girl ain't here, Malk. Not out back neither. Miss Tate probably sent her off to relatives. Come on. Let's clear out."

Eliza held her aim. "Listen to your baby brother, Cline boy."

Malcolm was the first out the door. He stopped in the tiny yard and screamed back, "Don't think for a minute we won't find her. We'll be watching."

Eliza rested the musket butt on her foot. "So will I." She pointed a knuckle at Malcolm. "Especially watching you."

Once the men were some distance from the house, Eliza shut the door, took in several deep breaths, and waited to stop trembling. She walked to their double cupboard, opened it, and pushed aside hanging coats.

Snook hopped out and hugged Eliza tightly around her waist as Eliza ran her hands all over Snook's scalp, shoulders, and arms. They remained silent for a long time, swaying in a mother-daughter slow dance.

"I was scared, Mama."

"Me too, baby. Terribly scared. I wouldn't be surprised if those thugs show back up here hiding under hoods and sheets."

Snook pulled back. "Why would they do that?"

Eliza shook her head while reviewing decades of ugliness she had witnessed. "It's complicated. A mean story. We'll talk about it some other time."

"What are we gonna do?"

Eliza kissed Snook's forehead. "We sure can't stay in this hollow, Snookie. We could sneak away to Cousin Susan's in Charlotte."

"I'm sorry, Mama. This is all my fault."

Eliza fell to her knees so that their heads were even. "Listen. You did nothing wrong. You're curious. You're imaginative. Those aren't bad. Those are good. Promise me, you'll stay true to who you are."

21. TUESDAY NIGHT IRREGULARITIES

Lance hid behind a Red Cedar shrub at the end of Trisha's porch. When she approached, he frightened her by whispering her name as he leapt out from nowhere.

Trisha jumped and crossed her hands over her chest. "Goodness, Lance. Never ever do that to me."

Lance motioned to follow him into darker shadows. "I thought you would be home before now. Where were you?"

Catching her breath, Trisha appeared proud as she announced, "We were at church."

"On a Tuesday evening?"

Trisha leaned against the porch edge, still trying to stop shaking. "We have a visiting pastor. He's holding nightly services."

Lance appeared apprehensive. "What's his name?"

Trisha enunciated with pride. "Pastor Flackman."

Lance joined Trisha leaning against the porch edge and shut his eyes. "I don't want you listening to that man."

Trisha spoke with even greater pride. "He's wonderful. Opening everybody's eyes to a miracle."

Lance spun around and slapped the porch floor. "You mean he's brainwashing everybody. That charlatan lies. He's dangerous."

"You're misjudging him. Go to his service with me tomorrow night."

"What kind of miracle? Is my cousin part of his so-called miracle?"

"Being part of a miracle is a good thing, Lance. A blessing. You should be honored Snook is a member of your family."

Lance shouted, "She's eight-years-old."

"Sssh." Trisha checked to assure her neighbors' porch light had not flipped on. "Last week, Snook was so excited talking with me. Can't you be happy for her?"

"There are people in this valley who want her dead."

Seeing the puzzled expression on Trisha's face, Lance felt he might as well have told her snow storms moved from winter to summer months.

Trisha snagged his arm. "You're making no sense. People don't want her dead. Snook's a saint—maybe a prophet. Special. Me and you always knowed that. Now everybody does."

Lance gripped Trisha's shoulders as if poised to shake her. "Listen to yourself. You're the one making no sense."

Trisha pulled away and placed her arms on her hips like her teachers did when stressing a point. "No miracle ever makes sense, Lance. They just exist. Cause God commands them."

"I get that, Trisha. Always have. But this ain't one of them times. Folks in Cline Town are calling what she is doing witchcraft. Curses of Satan. It's not a curse or a miracle, Trisha. It's over-active imagination of a wonderful little girl."

"No Lance. It's far more. I feel sorry you don't see that. Sorry you are turning your back on God."

Lance pounded the porch with his fist. "Oh my gosh. Not everything in yours and my life is about God."

Trisha resumed her stance of hands-on-hips. "Yes Lance. Everything is about God. Quit letting your stubborn talking get in your way. Open your heart."

Lance backed away and glared at Trisha. "You told them, didn't you?"

"Told who what?"

"About the cave. Her tree palace. You told them."

Trisha backed down from looking stern. "Pastor Flackman commanded us to share all we know."

"Oh my God."

"Don't use God's name as profanity."

"You have no clue to the damage you've done. You just assured Eliza and Snook ain't safe."

"God chose her, Lance. It's part of His plan."

"I'm gonna make arrangements and then tomorrow, I'm taking 'em both as far away from you and this hateful valley as I can."

Trisha's heart was so packed with joy and miracles, she ignored that Lance had sprinted away, failed to realize he neither kissed her nor spoke parting words.

22. GOLDEN GUARDIAN

Once her mother had assured doors were bolted and that she would be within arm's reach of the musket, Snook climbed in bed with her.

Snook was amazed that within moments, her mother was calmly sleeping as if the world were at peace. Her own mind, however, was galloping with memories of the Cline assault and investigating the cave and the rock messaging her.

She pictured the exact spot where she had stored the family's flashlight, pictured climbing into the cave's mouth, pictured the seven turns she must crawl through to arrive at the stone, and pictured a current of power flowing from the rock into her outstretched hands.

She did not know what images were waiting for her to receive, but pledged to not abandon the valley without one last immersion into earth's wisdom.

She trembled at the thought of leaving the bed where she and her mother's body were touching just enough to feel one another breathing. She feared straying into the hallway. Feared entering the room where she hid in darkness while listening to the confrontation. Feared sneaking along the street where the Clines may be staked out and watching. Feared navigating the woods in the night.

What could keep her safe? She could not take Mr. Gammon or Twinkles with her. Her notebook and crayons were essential but offered no protection.

She eased away from her mother's side and stared where moonlight streamed through a sliver between the curtains. She could make out the outline of her mother's dressing bureau and a glimmer of gold resting in its assigned position. The gift from her father to her mother.

The necklace and pendant embedded with love. The totem marking the start of her life.

The necklace would protect her.

She tiptoed to the vanity. Using her finger, she slid the necklace across dark mahogany until it toppled into her palm. It was so dainty that she could barely sense its existence, and yet, it loomed massive in her sense of feeling protected.

She had no doubt her mother would panic upon discovering that she and the necklace were absent, but she had no choice. She had a mission. Time was limited. There was no room for failure.

As she slipped past the houses, she realized that it was evening, but she had no watch or clock to know the exact time. All houses remained dark except a few at the end of the street where miners were returning from or leaving for shifts.

The last house before diverting into the woods was Olsen's home. At least at this hour, he would not be sitting on his porch ready to spring out and demand to join her for whatever adventure was on the day's docket.

She was pleased the mid-sky moon provided enough light that she did not need to flick on her flashlight and risk unmasking her mission.

An hour later, she reached the clearing and scaled her makeshift ladder to the lowest giant branch of the oak. From there, the tree provided all footholds and handholds necessary to ascend to her temple.

The roof remained unfinished, allowing her to enjoy moon and stars. She felt safe on her perch and content knowing the cave entrance would be visible once dawn approached. This was her domain and an invincible energy shielded her.

She ran her fingers over the pendant resting beneath her blouse, slid it up, and over and off her head. She gently twirled it in moonlight, imagining her father grinning as he presented it to her mother. She could picture his face, but only from stealing looks at his photo tucked away in a bureau drawer.

The scene she was imagining was richer than the one Hollywood movie romance she had seen, and the soundtrack was the symphony of nature's night creatures chirping and buzzing around her tower in the sky.

She suspended the necklace on a nail she had pounded halfway into a wall where she hoped to one day hang a flower basket.

Curled up on the floor, she stared up at her guardian token swaying in the light breeze.

After a few deep breaths, she was asleep.

23. WHERE'S UP?

Snook woke with sunlight flickering between branches and a finch chirping a courting song. She rubbed her eyes and sat up to orient to her surroundings.

The sun was above the horizon enough that she panicked. Had she wasted too much of the day?

She checked below to assure she was alone in the forest-bordered clearing, and then removed her sweater, slipped on her sneakers, slid on her backpack, descended through the oak limbs, and scurried down her ladder.

She hid behind the oak trunk, surveyed if anyone was invading her territory, darted to the cave entrance, and peeked out from behind two boards she had left in place.

All clear.

She vaulted through the cave's vestibule, feeling safe once the ceiling was low enough to require crawling and dark enough to require flicking on her flashlight.

At that same moment, overlooking the Winding Gulf tipple, Malcolm Cline threatened and quizzed his nephew about Snook. He learned that a classmate, Olsen Nielsen, had boasted at school about accompanying Snook to a special cave.

Malcolm's hands became shaky and he felt his heart accelerate. "Where's this Olsen Nielsen kid live?"

His nephew mumbled as he always did when Malcolm intimidated him. "Upper end of Winding Gulf. With his Grandma Nielsen."

Olsen was on his porch waiting for anyone to pass who would want to play or talk. His grandmother had left him to "guard the fort" as she always referred to the chore.

When Malcolm and his crew ascended onto the porch and asked if he was Olsen, the boy perked up, excited over the prospect of an opportunity beyond rolling toy cars across his porch.

He did not expect to have his shirt collar clutched and pulled so tight that he was strangling.

Malcolm's words were accompanied by spit hitting Olsen in the face. "Do you know Snook Tate?"

With restricted air, Olsen could only mutter. "Uh-huh."

"Do you know where she is?"

Olsen quivered as if a seizure were emerging. "Nuh-uh."

Malcolm released Olsen. "Do you know where her cave is?"

Olsen rubbed his throat and coughed. "I get lost easy."

Malcolm grabbed and twisted Olsen's arm. "Point which way or I'll break it."

Olsen pointed at the sky.

Malcolm turned to his gang, hoping for clarification, but they only shrugged. Malcolm released his hold on Olsen and shoved the boy's face down onto the wicker couch. "What the hell does pointing up mean?"

Olsen rubbed his aching arm and wheezed. "West?"

Malcolm huffed disgust. "What a dumb, puggy, little useless punk."

Olsen did not know Malcolm, but being labeled—even by the meanest man he had ever met—hurt his feelings more than being choked. He began to sob.

Malcolm's co-worker, Charlie Metcalf, ran onto Olsen's porch. "Hey Malcolm. I learnt Lance's girl Trisha knows the cave's location. It's the old Mitchell mine up on the ridge. She claims Snook built some kind of temple up there."

Malcolm tucked in his shirt and tightened his belt. With a smug face, he slowly descended from the porch. "Well fellas, I'd say this calls for going all out. We're gonna have ourselfs a little gathering."

24. BURLAP

Within the hour, Malcolm led a short packhorse out from his Uncle Dwight's stable.

Dwight spotted him through his kitchen window and bolted outside. "Malcolm? What the heck? You stealing Rosie?"

"Borrowing Rosie. Have her back by sundown."

"You could have the decency to ask."

Malcolm packed chewing tobacco into his mouth while his uncle glared, and then continued forward, met up with his younger brother Langdon, and led Rosie to the nearest colliery supply shed.

While Langdon stood guard, Malcolm slipped in and back out of the shed, toting two canvas sacks. The larger sack appeared it could be stuffed with soft fabric or rolled-up newspapers.

Langdon glared at the sack with suspicion. "What are you doing?"

Malcolm strapped the larger sack onto Rosie's back. "Nothing you need know about."

"You just stole coal company property."

"Not theirs no more. It's mine now."

"You'll get us arrested or shot for—"

"Shut your trap and hand me that little sack by your foot. Easy with it. It's breakable."

The brothers led Rosie to Olsen's house and turned westward toward the woods. Although many Winding Gulf citizens had frowned at the Cline brothers passing by with a packhorse, none frowned larger than Olsen who took a fierce stance on his porch with his chest puffed out. Malcolm yelled, "Boo," and Olsen ducked behind the wicker couch. Malcolm laughed louder than an entire coal-camp movie-house audience and then hocked a loogie into Olsen's yard.

A hundred yards into the woods, Malcolm and Langdon rendezvoused with two of Malcolm's drinking buddies: Pete and Charlie.

Pete held up a burlap potato sack. "Don't see why you insisted we bring these."

Malcolm spit brownish chew into a patch of weeds. "Cause it's daytime, idiot."

Pete whined, "Nobody wears Klan robes in the daytime."

Having a pot-belly stomach, Malcolm had easily become short of breath. "The Klan marches in daylight all the time. Ain't you never seen photos of them marches in D.C.? Sides, you want nutcases identifying you?"

Pete blocked Malcolm's path. "Nobody never goes up there to see nobody, Malk. Sides, we ain't doing nothing bad. Just talking to Snook. Scare a little sense into her. Don't need Klan robes for that."

Malcolm shoved Pete aside and resumed leading Rosie uphill.

An hour later, Malcolm paused at the edge of the clearing and donned his Klan robe.

Pete threw his robe-containing sack onto the ground. "It's hot out here. Plum asinine. I ain't wearing it."

Charlie followed suit and slung his sack behind a log.

Malcolm tugged his white hood over his head. "You dumbasses suit yourselfs. Let folks spot you and throw your dumb asses in jail."

Charlie selected a viewpoint at the front end of the clearing. "I'll keep lookout."

Langdon and Pete strolled to the base of the oak.

With his mouth agape, Pete stared up at the tree temple. "Will you look at that? Never seen nothing like that fore."

Malcolm guided Rosie to the mine entrance and while

examining it, yelled over his shoulder. "You two climb that oak and see if she's hiding out up there."

Pete cupped his hands and hollered, "Snook? You up there, honey?"

Malcolm kicked a loose rock. "I didn't order you to invite her to a tea party. I ordered you to climb that tree and look for her."

Langdon nodded to Pete. "I'll stand guard down here. You climb up."

Pete smirked. "You afraid of heights?"

Langdon's sudden beads of sweat revealed the truth. "I ain't afraid of no heights. But you climb up."

Pete chuckled and climbed while Langdon nervously scanned the forest and Malcolm peeped between boards into the cave.

Once Pete arrived inside the tree structure, he admired the craftsmanship, ran his hands over smoothed boards, and examined boards fitting tight. He yelled to the others. "She must have had help. No little girl built this by herself."

Malcolm screamed, "Is she there, you idiot?"

Pete yelled back. "Her sweater's here. And a necklace. She's gotta be close by."

Malcolm mumbled to himself. "Good. She's inside this dang blasted cave." He yelled across the clearing. "Charlie? Anybody coming?"

Charlie yelled back, "If they are, they been hearing you three clowns clear as day."

By the time Pete joined Langdon and they walked to Malcolm, Malcolm was stooped over running encased wires from the cave outside to a spot halfway to the oak.

Langdon gasped. "What the fuck you doing? You dynamiting this cave?"

Malcolm sounded calmer than Langdon ever remembered hearing his brother. "That's what it looks like, right? I'm gonna seal up this evil tunnel to the underground forever."

Malcolm stood erect and yanked off his hood. "Too hot out here for this blame thing." He pointed at the packhorse. "See that little sack dangling off Rosie's side? Inside's a jar of gasoline. Give that treehouse a soaking. Burn it along with that damn tree."

Langdon grabbed his brother's shoulder. "What if the girl's inside the cave, Malk?"

Malcolm shoved his brother's arm aside, kneeled beside the wires, and began connecting a small detonator. "So? What if she is?"

25. CRUMB SQUABBLING

When Eliza woke, mid-day sun was illuminating an area of wall above the curtain hooks.

She was stunned she had slept so late, but not surprised Snook was up and about. Even as a toddler, Snook had been an early riser.

Eliza took her time waking, splashing water on her face, and making her bed. Her husband had been a stickler for making the bed first thing. "An Army habit," Frederik had said. Now her habit, a way to feel he was close by.

She slid toward the kitchen in bedroom shoes several sizes too big—they had been Frederik's. She started coffee brewing, peeked in Snook's room, in the living room, and in on Mr. Gammon and Twinkles in the laundry room, believing Snook would be in there teasing them.

But she was not.

There were no rooms left to check.

Cold chills attacked Eliza's entire body.

Surely, Snook was not flaunting she was at home by presenting herself on the porch. Eliza rushed to peek out a front window. Snook's bike was there leaning against a post, but no sign of Snook.

Was she wandering around Winding Gulf despite the brutal confrontation last night? Please God no.

Maybe she went to Olsen's. Actually, that would be the last place she would go.

The best chance was Snook sought out Lance.

Lance resembled Frederik. Same features. Same voice. Same gestures. And now Lance was twenty: the age Frederik was when he proposed to her. Maybe that was why she and Snook felt content around Lance, felt complete trust in him.

She picked up the phone receiver to call Lance and recognized Jenny Mayfield and Shirley Hoskins gossiping on their party line. In past times of politely asking to interrupt their day-long phone conversations, they had spread word throughout Winding Gulf that she was rude. But her reputation was insignificant today. Today, she had to worry about their lives. Calling on the party line was risky. If she talked, the two women would eavesdrop and report that Snook had strayed from the house. If she called Lance and he mentioned Snook's whereabouts, Jenny Mayfield could blab that information to her Cline relatives.

If she left the house, there were other risks. Although never proven, the rumor mill insinuated that Malcolm Cline had set fire to the home of a family who had accused him of molesting their daughter. Fortunately, no one died in the fire, but neighbors refused to associate with the displaced family out of fear of Cline Town retaliation. The homeless family not only fled the county, they returned to Mexico. When state police officials had questioned county locals, the answer was the typical lie: Ku Klux Klan members from another county or another state had passed through and set the house ablaze.

Eliza sat in her living-room maple rocker, a wedding gift from Frederik's parents. She was too paralyzed to rock.

She heard a thud outside on the porch and peeped out, fearing arsonists were at work. But two finches were determined to snatch the same crumb resting beneath a chair. She spotted other crumbs, but the birds remained fixated on fighting over that specific crumb.

She returned to her rocker and heard a knocking sound. "Stubborn little birds." After sitting minutes more, she heard the sound a second time, but this time recognized it was not embattling birds; it was a faint knock. She opened the door and there stood Olsen. "Oh, my goodness. I thought you were two little birds squabbling."

Olsen looked in every direction, but did not see any birds. Whatever his thoughts were about the birds, those thoughts evaporated as if they had never occurred and he turned to Eliza. "Mean men are searching for Snook."

Eliza squatted to be at Olsen's height. "What mean men?"

"They hurt my throat and neck." Olsen pulled back his collar for Eliza to see red marks.

"Oh my gosh. Come in, come in. Quick." She shut the door. "I'll wrap ice in a cloth and hold it to your throat."

"Thank you very much. I appreciate that."

Whatever awful things Snook had said about Olsen, he certainly seemed to be well-mannered.

Olsen jumped when the cold cloth touched his raw skin, and Eliza winced as if she had hurt her own body. "Sorry. Here. You hold it the way it feels best."

Olsen gently patted the cloth to his neck.

Eliza waited a moment before asking, "Who were the mean men that did this to you?"

"I only heard one of 'em's name. Malcolm."

Eliza felt dizzy and sat, feeling afraid to hear more. "How do you know they are searching for Snook?"

"They asked where Snook's cave is and I pointed west." Olsen pointed his finger at the ceiling. "But Snook said that way's up. The men got angrier. Said I confused them."

Eliza was unclear what Olsen's explanation meant, but had no doubt her daughter was in danger. "Do you know if Snook went to her cave?"

Olsen appeared on the verge of crying. "No ma'am. Not for certain."

Eliza patted his knee. "Good job, Olsen. You're a brave

young man coming here. I'm proud of you."

Olsen began sobbing.

Eliza was sure the boy had been holding back, waiting to feel safe before he let loose. "Is there anything I can get you?"

Still crying, Olsen muttered, "A Baby Ruth?"

Eliza grinned and retrieved a candy bar from their cookie jar, feeling Olsen was going to be fine. But Snook? Her mind was filled with awful stories she had heard about Cline Town and Malcolm Cline and the Ku Klux Klan.

Without knocking, the front door swung open and Eliza and Olsen both yelped and grabbed onto whatever piece of furniture was closest.

It required a moment to realize the intruder was Lance.

He was out of breath. "Is she here?"

After a moment of paralysis, Eliza shook her head.

Although Olsen's mouth was full of Baby Ruth, he managed to mumble, "She could be at her tree palace." He swallowed and added, "Malcolm somebody and his men headed up there looking for her."

26. ALLEN FOX LEGACY

Lance sped his pickup to his parents' house and grabbed a flashlight, a few simple tools, his uncle's full-face charcoal filtration mask, and a crowbar. He stuffed the items into an army duffle bag and tossed it into his pickup bed.

Today was the first time he had ever jogged toward Mitchell Ridge. He kicked into full gear, leaping over logs, ducking low hanging limbs, ignoring briars and even a copperhead in the middle of the crude trail.

He was a half-mile from the cave when he heard an explosion. He had grown up hearing black-powder and dynamite explosions, but it made no sense in 1959 to hear an explosion anywhere near that ridge.

He yearned to speed up his assent, but was already straining his legs and lungs to maximum capacity.

From his tree-palace-building time with Snook, he recognized when he was a hundred yards from the clearing. He eased forward with the caution of a sniper, hypervigilant of the woods, all the while inspecting the scorched tree. All leaves had burned away. Charred wood remained at the location where Snook's dream temple had reigned.

The oak skeleton spooked him. Had Snook been trapped in her tree palace?

He searched the tree line. Did he dare call out her name? Had the Cline gang spared her? Had they kidnapped her? Were they lying in wait?

He turned his attention from the massacred tree and encircling forest to the cave opening—or where there had once been an opening. It was now a pile of loose dirt and rocks with splintered timbers jutting out.

Lance often heard the expression that someone's heart

sank. Now, he experienced that accurate description and fell to his knees.

During the past week, he had felt angry at God, maybe even hated God. But staring at the explosion debris, he begged God for Snook to be uninjured, to be alive.

He approached the devastation and recalled when his seventh-grade classmate, Allen Fox, died in the mine. The mine entrance had been too tight to allow rescuers and equipment to reach the boy. Back in 1951, there was a second entrance around the side of the ridge with a dirt road that rescue vehicles accessed.

That road had washed away and that mine entrance had allegedly been sealed, but maybe there was a chance he could reach Snook.

Lance slung the duffle bag over his shoulder and headed the direction he hoped would lead him to Snook.

He used his bare hands and thinly clothed arms to whack weeds and briars dominating heavy undergrowth. Where terrain was too steep to walk erect, he crawled across moss clumps and pointed rocks.

He arrived at the second entrance where a rusting metal wall with a timber door intimidated him. The structure was as well-built and strong as any colliery building. The hinged door had a massive cut-proof padlock fastening it to a metal frame cemented into surrounding boulders. The barricade was secure enough that no keep-out sign had been necessary.

Even if he managed to pry off the lock—and dents in the door indicated that others had attempted such a feat and failed—would he be able to swing the door open? The hinges were obviously on the inside, meaning the door swung inward. Over the years, surely rocks and other debris had fallen and blocked the door.

What could he accomplish with a meager hammer and crowbar?

He approached the door and kneeled on soil packed hard enough it felt like cement. He positioned his hands in prayer as he had been taught as a child, feeling silly, thinking if anyone saw him, he would feel stupid. But once he closed his eyes and envisioned Snook wearing one of her many tomboy outfits, a plea flowed from his lips. He did not want to admit this was praying, but the moment resonated with childhood church and bedtime moments.

When he opened his eyes, he was a stronger man on a mission. That door was going to yield one way or another.

He positioned his crowbar into the giant lock and grunted while applying all his strength.

The lock snapped.

Pushing with his shoulder lodged against the door, it creaked open, scraping loose dirt and rocks like a road scraper until there was just enough room to squeeze inside.

He collapsed inside onto his back, cried for a moment, and flicked on his flashlight.

The fumes were strong enough that he quickly fitted the mask to his face.

He had no idea how far he must travel to reach Snook, but was relieved that the inside consisted of a corridor large enough to accommodate small vehicles.

He feared the corridor would bifurcate. Maybe once. Maybe numerous times. He risked getting lost. He risked his respirator mask failing. He risked discovering Snook was not in the cave. He risked finding Snook too late for her to be alive.

27. LEFT TURNS

Lance had only walked a hundred yards when the cave divided into two identical-appearing corridors. He reasoned that bearing left made sense as that would keep him on the same side of the mountain he had traversed outside. For safety, he shaped a handful of rocks on the cave floor to create an arrow indicating the way out.

The cave split two more times and he continued bearing left and marking his return route.

During his fourth leg of spelunking, he stumbled upon a cave in. If his reasoning was correct of bearing left, his only choice was to breakthrough that obstacle.

He shined his light near the ceiling and spotted a small gap, possibly large enough to wiggle through. Dragging his duffle bag, he climbed the pile of various sized rocks, inducing small avalanches, forcing him to grab onto larger rocks to keep from sliding.

Once on top, he shined his light into the cavity and was disheartened to find it crammed with small rocks. He tossed rock after rock behind him, hearing them create more sliding of the parent pile.

His sense of hope rested upon his feeling air gliding past his face from front to back. When he yelled, "Snook," into the forward blackness, his voice echoed, suggesting an open passage.

He wiggled forward several yards. Instead of his light illuminating debris within touching distance, it was shining past darkness and dimly illuminating a distant wall. He tossed a small rock into the abyss and within a second, heard it strike ground. He pulled himself forward with his elbows until he could peer downward. The steep slope of debris ended a few yards below, followed by level ground.

He body-surfed down the back side, feeling sharp rocks jab his ribs. If he was bleeding, he did not care. He could check his body later.

Once he was on steady ground, he proceeded forward, hoping he had not ripped his face mask. So far, the device was preventing lightheadedness and nausea.

He developed a routine of walking a hundred feet, stopping to remove his mask, yelling Snook's name, listening, replacing his mask, and continuing forward.

Although the cave narrowed, it remained large enough to remain upright. Shining his light forward and after rounding several bends, he recognized a slab of rock. It resembled Snook's prized find.

He yelled her name but received no answer. Was this the correct rock? If it was and she was not there, did that mean he would have to crawl to the original entrance? Was she trapped beneath dynamited debris?

Then he saw her body.

Motionless, but appearing to be breathing.

Lance dropped to his knees beside her, pulled off his mask, and gently shook her.

Snook opened her eyes. "Lance?" She coughed for a minute and then grabbed Lance's arm. "Daddy was here. He talked to me."

Lance brushed debris from her hair. "The fumes are getting to you. I need to get you out of here fast."

Snook clutched his head. "No Lance. Daddy really was here. He promised you would come and you did."

"We can share my mask."

"Me and you got important work to do."

Lance hugged Snook tightly and wept.

28. SMOKE

When Lance and Snook reached the edge of the woods near Olsen's house, Lance grabbed Snook's shoulder to prevent her from walking into the open. "Something's not right. I smell smoke. Not chimney or woodstove smoke."

Snook sniffed. "What is it?"

"Stay here a moment." Keeping low, Lance eased to his pickup parked on the street and ducked behind it. "Damn it." He was blindsided upon discovering all four tires were flat. He had no doubt Malcolm Cline was responsible.

Looking down the street, he jolted when he saw Snook and Eliza's home smoldering in ruins. A crowd of neighbors had gathered, staring at a still-standing chimney and shaking their heads.

Hunched over, Lance returned to Snook and sat. He gestured for her to sit with him and wrapped his arms around her. "I've got something to say and you have to promise to stay quiet. Cause if you make a sound, the people who dynamited you in that cave might hear and come for us. Can you do that?"

Snook paused a long moment. "Tell me."

"Your home was burned. Nothing's left."

Snook remained quiet while pondering practical matters of where she would sleep, eat, and store her belongings. Then it hit her; she had no belongings. Twinkles and Mr. Gammon had nowhere for her to feed them. Were they alive? Was her mother alive?

She seized Lance's arm tightly enough to hurt him. "Is Mama okay?"

Lance hugged her tighter. "I don't know, but if anyone has enough smarts to escape, it's your mom."

Snook sobbed hard while remaining silent, feeling the entire world was listening, expecting her to cry out.

There was still enough daylight that they could not chance approaching the smoking remnants and being spotted. Lance nodded toward Olsen's house. "How well do you know your little friend?"

Snook sniffed her nose clear and wiped her eyes. "He's like an irritating, pesky little brother."

"Do you trust him with secrets?"

"Only cause his memory ain't worth a hill of beans."

Lance chuckled at Snook's honesty. "Who else lives there?"

"His grandma."

"How's her memory?"

"Worse."

"Good. Let's sneak you into their house."

When Olsen opened the door and saw Snook, he overflowed with excitement and tried to hug her, but she shoved him away.

"Snook? You ain't gonna believe what happened. Twenty men—maybe forty—tried to choke me and kill me if I didn't tell 'em where our cave was."

Lance whispered, "I thought he had poor memory."

Snook waved Lance to keep away. "What did you tell them twenty or forty men?"

"The truth. That I get lost easy." Olsen sniffed the air. "What's that smoke smell?"

Lance gave Snook the thumbs-up sign. "Stay safe."

Once Snook was situated with a boy who was clueless that a house on his street had burned, Lance set about locating Eliza.

He felt certain his Aunt Eliza had the good sense to avoid public places, but was baffled where she would hold up.

29. WAS NEVER HERE

Lance could not stop thinking Eliza may have died in the fire, but did not dare show his face at the burned-out shell of a house to ask spectators. Too many people were hunting them.

Lance eliminated Eliza's brother's and two sisters' homes as places she would have gone. Malcolm would definitely search those first. Lance selected Eliza's best friend Teresa as a possibility.

Teresa appeared frightened as she answered the door, quickly leaning out to scan the street and motioning with a flapping hand for him to hurriedly enter. "It's not safe for you to come here."

Lance proceeded farther inside away from windows. "Every spot in this valley is dangerous for me. I have four flat tires to prove it." He stepped into the hallway where no one from outside could see him. "Do you know where my Aunt Eliza is?"

Teresa closed the kitchen curtains and motioned for him to enter. "She came here and left Snook's pets during the fire. Said she didn't want to endanger me by telling me where she was going. Malcolm barged in here and almost broke my wrist twisting it. Then he and his gang got into it with Johnny's gang on the street. Shots were fired—right in front of my porch. Johnny's gang carried somebody away. Everybody was screaming and fighting over Snook. Don't make sense."

None of this does, Lance thought, but did not speak. Instead, he sat, raised his shirt, and checked his ribs. A small jagged-rock wound was oozing blood.

Teresa hurried to the bathroom and returned with a World-War-Two Army tin medical box, gifted to her by her father. She pulled out cotton, rubbing alcohol, and a box of various size bandages. She cleaned and bandaged Lance as they talked. "Eliza fears Snook is dead."

Lance winced as the alcohol stung. "Snook had a close call, but she's hanging in there. Somebody—I'm guessing Malcolm—dynamited the old mine entrance with Snook inside. Torched her treehouse."

"Lord have mercy." After spotting a blood spot seeping through, Teresa added a second bandage atop the first. "Winding Gulf—this entire run—seen its fair share of violence and deaths. Never lets up. Wish I'd joined folks years ago who refused to put up with it and high-tailed it out."

She packed items back into her Army tin. "But that cost money most of us don't have."

Lance checked the bandage and nodded *well done*. "You got any hunch where Aunt Eliza would go?"

Teresa talked while pouring each of them a glass of orange Kool-aid. "She didn't say, but I know she's sentimental about what's left of her Grandmother Earl's old house up the hill from the colliery tipple buildings. Also sentimental about Frederick's Grandmother Tate's house above where the old colored school stood. I tagged along with her several times to tend flower patches at both. Worth trying those."

Lance swigged his drink. "Thanks Teresa. If anyone asks, I was never here."

30. APPLES

Lance avoided the road leading to the colliery and trudged parallel through undergrowth to avoid being seen. Near the colliery, he turned uphill and climbed a rarely used road to reach the old Earl house.

He had not viewed the premise in years and was stunned by vines strangling the house as if binding it from completely falling apart.

Once Lance traipsed through knee-high fireweed, he was drawn to an apple core on the porch's bottom step. He was no sleuth, but recognized bits of apple clinging to the stem were still moist. He looked for other traces of recent human presence and found cigarette butts that were still dry; it had rained two days earlier.

Could be a sign kids had been smoking while camping out for a haunted-house experience. Or kids sneaking into the ruins to drool over porn. He suddenly recalled Eliza's distaste for smoking. Those could not be her stubs.

There were a few tin cans that obviously had been used for target practice. Windows had no glass left for kids to shoot out, but he spotted slugs embedded in wooden siding.

He entered, testing the strength of floor boards by tapping his heel on each without bearing weight on them. All boards creaked but held. That noise ended any chance of him sneaking up on someone.

An old cabinet had come loose from the wall and crashed onto the floor long enough ago that an inch of dust and debris covered it.

There was bird crap staining overhead rafters and the carcass of a rat lay in one corner.

Sunlight flickered through multiple holes in the roof and a set of rusted bedsprings lay in front of the fireplace, probably dragged from a bedroom by kids camping out or making out.

Something caught his eye. Maybe he was a sleuth after all. Almost hidden from view behind a collapsed chair was a metal flush-pull-door handle in the floor. It was difficult to make out the corresponding outline cut into the floor, but a trapdoor definitely was there. He remembered a similar curiosity at a grade-school-friend's home. The trapdoor led to an apple cellar that had no other entrances and no windows. Two-feet-thick stone walls kept the cellar at a steady cool temperature year-round.

He kneeled and examined the handle closer. Although the floor was coated with dust, the small metal handle was clean. It must have recently been used.

Lance gently tugged on the handle, swinging open one end of the rectangular-shaped hatch a few inches.

A woman's voice calmly and firmly sounded from darkness below. "Open that one inch more and I'll blow your fucking hand off."

Lance let go and the trapdoor slammed shut.

Lance slid backwards a couple of feet. "Aunt Eliza? It's me. Lance."

Eliza yelled, "Who's with you?"

"Nobody. Just me. Lance."

"Is Snook safe?"

"She is now. I left her with Olsen."

Eliza shoved the trapdoor upward. Her voice sounded alarmed. "Oh my God. You left Snook with Olsen? How is that possibly safe?"

"There's no one else I trust that Malcolm and his thugs aren't watching."

Eliza climbed up the ladder and half-way out of the pit. "We've gotta get her outta there."

Lance extended a helping hand. "We've gotta get both of you outta this valley. Better if we get you all the way outta this state."

Eliza hugged Lance, the first time either remembered hugging the other in years.

Eliza whispered into Lance's ear as if the bullet-ridden walls were eavesdropping. "I know a place we can go, but I can't telephone to ask. At least not call on no Winding Gulf party line."

31. CLUB COUPE

Lance borrowed a 1947 Oldsmobile Club Coupe from Ole Lady Hawkesberry as she was known, an elderly widow who had not driven for years and for whom Lance often performed yard work and gutter cleaning for free.

The car had garnered enough dust from lack of use that he believed he could drive it without heads turning.

Lance and Eliza slipped into Olsen and his grandmother's house without knocking.

Olsen stood in the corner, watching Eliza and Snook hug, touching every inch of one another until Lance physically pulled them apart. "We need to go."

Eliza whispered into Snook's ear. "No one can know we was here. It would be unconscionable to place these good people in harm's way."

Snook shed a sweater Olsen lent her and handed it to him, but he returned it. "I got plenty others. Grandmommie knits all day long. You want tea or milk or Coke or something?"

"Thanks Olsen, but we gotta leave."

"Where you going?"

"Listen. We aren't really here. Tell people who ask about us that we weren't never here."

"But you are here."

Snook pondered Olsen's style of thinking. "Tell 'em you saw me, but I weren't really here. That will be enough truth and also confuse them. Got it?"

Olsen frowned puzzlement, his most frequent expression. "Uh-huh."

Olsen walked them to the door and tugged on Snook's shoulder. "Can I hug you goodbye?"

"I'd let you, but I'm not really here. Remember? Bye."

Olsen appeared even more perplexed.

Eliza and Snook stretched out on the Oldsmobile's rear seat and hid beneath a wool blanket, placing Twinkles and Mr. Gammon on the floor. Lance wore a wool-sock hat, striving to be unrecognizable, yearning to yank it off the moment they reached Sophia since it made his scalp and neck itch.

While stopped in Sophia, Eliza used a payphone to call her cousin Susan in Charlotte, North Carolina and ask if she and Snook could visit for an undetermined length of time.

Susan was concerned about the suddenness but delighted to have them visit, boasting about the wonders of city living.

Earlier in Winding Gulf, when their house had been afire, Eliza had the forethought to snatch her money cache before escaping. She was able to purchase two tickets from the Prince Train Station to Charlottesville, Virginia and from there onward to Charlotte.

Standing on the Prince Train Station platform, Snook hugged Lance farewell and began sobbing.

"Whoa." Lance gently pushed her back to arm's length and looked her in the eye. "Look at me, kid."

After a moment, Snook looked.

"You're my tough soldier gal. I seen you conquer a million grueling challenges."

Crying launched hiccups such that Snook struggled speaking. "Me and you suffered through lots together, Lance."

"We sure did, didn't we? Me and you, kid? Comrades for life. Nobody can't never take that away and one thing for sure, nobody's gonna believe our story. But it's all true."

Snook hugged tighter than before. "You're always here when I need anything. Now you won't be."

"Tell you what. I'm gonna stay a bit in Beckley with

Shirley, my old high-school flame—if she'll have me. I'll hire some kid to drive Ole Lady Hawkesberry's car back to Winding Gulf, and if everything works out—and you don't mind terrible—I'll join you and Aunt Eliza down in Charlotte. Hunt for a car-mechanic job. It's what I always dreamed to do anyhow. What do you think?"

"How soon?"

Lance kissed Snook on the forehead. "Soon as I can, kid."

"Promise?"

"Cross my heart and hope to die."

Lance waited until he could no longer hear the train heading eastward toward Charlottesville, and with hands in pockets, he meandered toward the Oldsmobile.

32. GYMNATORIUM

Neighbors pressured Olsen's grandmother to attend Pastor Flackman's evening worship service, emphasizing she must bring Olsen.

The faithfuls—as Flackman referred to them—had increased in number such that he requested—a polite euphemism—the school board to allow him to use the school's gymnatorium.

All folding chairs on the gym floor were occupied, forcing Olsen, his grandmother, and a dozen other attendees to stand in back.

Flackman raised his hand with palms turned upward. "Welcome, welcome brothers and sisters on this lovely evening that Mother Earth provided for us."

Olsen squirmed, irritated the man stole the words *Mother Earth* from Snook.

Flackman scooted a flip chart to face the gathering. "As you see, even though we barely got started, donations are growing. In a week or two, we will be able to lay foundations for our temple at the site of the cave—if each of you recruit one more donor. God bless you."

A murmur of determination and satisfaction rippled throughout the attendees.

"The earth's heart sang and we listened. Our mission is prospering."

The group sing-songed together, "Praise for Mother Earth and to God. Amen."

"Yes, my friends. We are on a virtuous path. And tonight, we have a special treat. Do you know who blessed us with his presence?"

Members rotated their heads surveying the room and whispering to one another.

"Anybody? Anybody know?"

All shook their heads no.

Flackman chuckled, rubbing his palms together with eagerness. "We have Prophet Jessica's friend with us." Flackman motioned with an open palm toward Olsen. "Our very own Olsen Nielsen."

Olsen's lower jaw dropped as if he were a trout trying to swallow dangling bait.

Attendees shifted in their seats to stare at him with shorter adults half-standing for a better view.

Olsen pressed his face into his grandmother's sweatered side. She yanked his head with both hands and twisted his face toward the crowd. "Don't be rude, Olsen."

Olsen's face reddened and his eyes watered.

Flackman gestured for the boy to approach. "Good people want to see you. Hear from you."

A girl from Olsen's class—a head taller—clutched Olsen's hand and towed him upfront.

Flackman stared down at Olsen with the body language of a king commanding from a throne. "Welcome, my son. We are eager to learn from you."

Olsen faced his admirers, shading his eyes with his hand.

"Don't be shy. We know you and Prophet Jessica were close. Know you must be suffering unfathomable pain from her absence."

The crowd moaned sympathetic *aahs* and displayed dramatized grief with hands over hearts.

"Tell us. When was the last time you viewed our wondrous prophet?"

"What?" Olsen muttered.

"The last time you saw Jessica Rae Tate."

"Uh." Olsen froze.

"Go on. You're among loving friends here. When was the last time?"

Olsen glanced at his grandmother, at the girl who had

dragged him to the torturous spot, at his feet, and then mumbled, "Wednesday."

Flackman bent over so that his head was even with Olsen's. "A bit louder. You can do better. I know you can."

Olsen spoke slightly louder. "Wednesday."

"Wednesday." Flackman appeared puzzled. "Now would that be this recent Wednesday, or would that be the Wednesday from the previous week?"

Olsen mumbled, "Previous week."

The crowd gasped and whispered to one another.

Flackman stood erect and spoke as if translating a foreign language. "Young Mr. Nielsen here reports he witnessed Prophet Jessica on that very Wednesday, the day her house burned." Flackman stepped closer to his followers and waved his pointing finger in the air. "The same Wednesday the holy cave was desecrated with the prophet inside."

Flackman circled on the rostrum several times before facing the congregation, abruptly kneeled, grabbed Olsen by his shoulders so they were nose to nose, and yelled in his face. "Is it possible you saw Prophet Jessica after the house burned and the cave exploded?"

Crowd murmurs rose in volume to an agitated pitch.

Flackman waved his hands at the crowd. "Calm. Calm. We must remain calm."

The crowd required a moment to quieten.

"Now young man. That Wednesday—from the week before—the day Jessica Rae Tate disappeared in the cave." Flackman held his hand over his heart. "Yes or no? And remember, you are compelled to speak the truth. Did you lay eyes on Jessica Rae Tate later than those tragic events?"

Olsen nodded.

"And where was that sighting?"

Olsen talked to his shoes. "Our house."

Crowd rumbling intensified and Flackman again calmed them with gestures. He returned to Olsen. "So, you actually saw her? Jessica?"

"Uh-huh."

"She was there at your house?"

"Not really."

People turned to one another, frowning and gesturing that they were confused.

"Explain what you mean so we may understand."

Olsen inhaled deeply and blew out air as if he meant it to strike the back row. "I saw her there, but she wasn't really there."

Flackman put his hand on Olsen's shoulder and spoke loudly while over-enunciating to assure every human in the room understood him as if he were a lawyer stressing his main point to a jury. "So, you saw her."

Olsen nodded.

"But she was not there."

Olsen nodded.

"Thank you, Olsen." Flackman gently pushed Olsen aside and gestured with fluttering fingers for him to scurry to his grandmother.

Olsen sprinted to his grandmother and buried his face in her chest.

Flackman paused for a dramatic moment of puckering his lips, rubbing his chin, scratching his scalp, and then speaking in his loudest voice to the crowd and beyond. "Folks. There you have it. From the mouth of babes. Honesty. Truth. Revelations."

He paced back and forth before continuing.

"Olsen saw the girl prophet ... and yet ... she was not there."

He paced another round before continuing.

"And how is that possible?" Flackman pounded his fist on the lectern top. "Because what this boy saw was a vision. A vision. Jessica Rae Tate is no longer with us. And yet she is. She is not dead in spirit. She is hidden. Watching us. Judging us. Guiding us. Crawling into our hearts. Into our souls. Each and every one of us are commanded to listen. Commanded to seek wisdom from this hidden saint. This hidden prophet. Her lessons are lessons of Mother Earth."

Olsen fled outside through the gymnatorium metal doors, shoving them open with force, allowing strong wind to flow into the room and scatter paper plates and napkins from the buffet table.

Flackman seized the moment. "Behold the breath of God."

33. CHARLOTTE

Snook resembled a scared puppy withdrawing into herself when confronted by Charlotte's stifling summer heat, twenty-story buildings, trolleys, neon signs, and perpetual traffic.

Snook, however, was enamored by the new Carnegie Library on North Tryon Street. After spending much time browsing, a librarian directed her to the children's books. Snook announced with confidence that she was interested in science books housed in the adult section. The librarian enjoyed Snook and they began a friendship that years later would lead to Snook inviting her to Mr. Gammon's backyard funeral service.

A month after their 1959 big move to Charlotte, Snook protested her mother dragging her into the office of the county clerk to seek changing their names, a task made onerous by having lost their birth certificates in the house fire, and the Raleigh County Clerk in Beckley dragging out supplying required records.

Eliza selected the name Margaret Frederik for herself. Since she was relinquishing *Tate*—her husband's last name—she was adamant about including his first name as part of her new identity.

She insisted Snook choose a new first name before school began. Snook boasted her name must be Rachel Carson Frederik, explaining that Rachel Carson was her favorite science author, her hero in environmentalism.

The first day of fourth grade, Snook was stunned to learn each classroom consisted of students who were all in the same grade. She was delighted the school library was a large room rather than a few dozen books housed in a closet as had been the case in Winding Gulf.

True to his word, Lance appeared within months and

sought car-mechanic work. He had barely begun when a co-worker introduced him to applying his skills to fine-tuning engines for stock car racing. He excelled and was soon invited to work with cars at the newly opening Charlotte Motor Speedway in nearby Concord.

Snook had never seen her cousin as excited as when discussing stock cars and the speedway. Over the next years, Lance thrilled to the speedway hosting major races of NASCAR and other national championship events.

He grew close to his team in the pit and to the woman he married who shared his love for racing and mechanics, making her a rock star with his crew.

His wife never pried into details about his early life in West Virginia, probably because Lance's face soured whenever she broached the topic.

He got by with new acquaintances by being vague about his upbringing, but detested how evading questions made him feel like a criminal on the lam.

From time to time, Lance telephoned Eliza's friend, Teresa, inquiring about Winding Gulf. He learned that the town's two religious factions grew and then dwindled in size and ferocity after months of shootings and two additional house burnings. The only fatality had been a local news reporter being at the wrong place at the wrong time.

Lance informed Eliza of news about Winding Gulf, hoping to curtail her desire to re-establish contact with relatives or other coal-camp inhabitants, but refrained from sharing all news with Snook.

Back in the 1920s, Winding Gulf had been the third-largest town in Raleigh County, but by the 1960s, the region's mines were gradually closing and people moving out. The writing was on the wall that the area would become a ghost town of rotting colliery buildings and weed-snared house foundations.

While Winding Gulf shrank to a few scattered houses, Snook thrived in Charlotte.

Although she enjoyed urban offerings, in her dreams, she continued to feast her eyes upon the gentle curves of the Appalachians, sit atop ridges watching hawks soaring in upward drafts, and join porch gatherings of banjo and juice-harp songfests.

The mountains had and always would call her.

34. DONE GOOD - 2024

In the spring of 2024, at age 63, Snook retired from teaching in the Department of Environmental Sciences and Engineering at the University of North Carolina in Chapel Hill.

Snook and her husband relocated to Charlotte, relishing weekends at their son's family cabin in the North Carolina mountains. Their Blowing Rock cabin sat atop a three-thousand-foot gneiss cliff overlooking the sweeping wilderness of the Johns River Gorge.

Snook's grandchildren delighted watching local wildlife interact with their grandmother. Sometimes, a fox sat on the bottom porch step beside Snook's feet, seeming to enjoy sharing the view of the smokey-blue ridges. A raccoon—named Raymond by their family—nightly waddled to Snook and held out its paw for a treat.

Snook's nine-year-old granddaughter, Audrey—named by Snook in honor of Audrey Hepburn—differed from her twin brothers and sister. Instead of racing outside to watch their grandmother mingle with animals, Audrey chose to stand alone at the far end of their narrow yard near a Fraser fir.

Snook observed Audrey from a distance, amazed by house finches alighting on the girl's outstretched finger, appearing to be addressing her.

Only once did Snook approach Audrey during a moment she was with a bird. "I may be wrong, but it appears to me that you and your little finch friends chat with one another."

Audrey answered with no change in emotion and without breaking eye contact with the bird. "Most people only hear her chirps. Not her talking. Most people can't hear those sounds."

Snook recalled science research about Zebra finches and the complexity of vocalizations. "What about you? Do you hear this and other birds talking?"

Audrey shrugged.

"What is she telling you?"

Audrey stared at the horizon. "A giant storm is coming. Not today. But soon."

She wiggled a finger in the finch's face and released it. "Mom's calling me. Excuse me."

Audrey returned inside while Snook sat, puzzled she had not heard Audrey being called. Was Audrey capable of hearing sounds most people could not?

She chuckled in private. If a rock can send messages, why not finches? Perhaps this particular grandchild had more in common with Snook than she had suspected.

She questioned Audrey's younger twin brothers about the matter. "Do you think your big sister talks with those birds she hangs out with?"

While pitching seeds for crows to fetch, the more assertive twin answered, "Nope."

Snook waited until her grandson looked her direction. "To me it looks likes Audrey listens to them. Talks with them."

The boy shook his head. "Audrey's plain weird."

"So crazy," the other twin added.

35. GRANDKIDS SNITCH

At age 75, following his wife's midsummer death in Charlotte, Lance's health rapidly declined. Snook helped him to move into Sunrise Senior Living.

Within weeks, Lance was transferred to the assisted-living wing and Snook began weekday visits. They progressed—or regressed—to holding one another's hands whenever they talked.

Lance grinned at her. "You're still my tough soldier gal." As he had done for over a half-century, he winked.

Most of Lance's interactions ended with bouts of coughing. "What I get for coal mining and smoking. Your mama warned me. I should have listened. Could have lasted another seventy-five years." He chuckled, followed by prolonged coughing.

Once Lance caught his breath, he stared into Snook's perpetually inquisitive eyes. "What's up with you? Some kind of giant award your grandkids told me."

Snook leaked a resigned smile. "I ordered the buggers to not brag."

"Good luck with that. They're proud of their grandma. Especially Audrey. She told me she wants to be a teacher like you. What award?"

Snook stalled, preferring to not talk about herself. "Lifetime Achievement Award."

Lance snickered, thinking about what he was about to say. "I awarded you that award five decades ago and bunches of times since."

Snook chuckled. "And vice versa."

"What's this one for, Professor Frederik?"

The way Lance pronounced Frederik revealed how after all these decades, he still had disdain for her name change.

"Well ..." Looking into her cousin's eyes, Snook realized stalling would not redirect his curiosity. "For my work in environmental sciences."

"Wow. That falls right in line with your lifetime missions. You must be pleased."

"Pleased more by knowing about the research my students are doing."

"Always unselfish. Who's giving you this award?"

Snook spoke quickly enough that her words ran together. "The American Academy of Environmental Engineers and Scientists."

"Holy crap." Lance tried to sit up but could not and gestured he would refuse help. "Imagine that. An entire nation awarding you."

Snook snickered. "Not an entire nation. A small specialized group of academicians."

"I still say holy crap."

Lance appeared pained while struggling to shift his back to another position. "I'm curious. With all your awards and promotions, what do you tell folks when they ask about your history, about you growing up?"

Snook shrugged. "I tell 'em I grew up in Charlotte."

"Hm."

"Partially true. A small lie I am able to live with."

Lance fell silent for a moment, thinking about his own deceitfulness, about never opening fully to his wife. "Grew up in Charlotte. Huh. Fact is, before Charlotte, you did more growing up than most people do in entire lifetimes." Lance squeezed his cousin's hand tighter. "You done good, kid. We both did." He rang his buzzer.

Snook jarred. "I'm right here. What do you need?"

"To be put on my bedpan. Love you as I do, some activities are off-limits. Besides, my nurse, Margie, is cute as a button."

A male nursing aid entered, showing off muscles that

were as large as if he pitched tree trunks in his spare time.

Lance shut his eyes and muttered, "Crap. Him again."

Snook leaned over and kissed Lance's forehead. "Love you."

"Love you too, kid. Congratulations Professor."

Snook smiled long enough that the nursing aid intervened. "Can you give us a minute?"

Lance and Snook smiled at one another, blew kisses, and waved farewell.

36. FRIENDS ARE FOREVER

Sitting on the stage in Memorial Hall, Snook listened with gleeful ears to a UNC student present her paper that had paved the path for the young woman to receive the Rachel Carson Healthy Planet Award during her senior year of high school. Her brief offering was followed by a visiting faculty member from UC-Berkeley, lecturing on her latest research in Geomicrobiology.

Following the two academic moments, a visiting professor from Rutgers, representing AEES, presented the lifetime achievement award to Snook. Snook went deaf as the professor reviewed her accomplishments in academics and research. She slipped into thinking more private thoughts about family life and treasures in her life, stories she never revealed, not even when interrogated by the press.

A colleague on the stage beside her, nudged her elbow when time came for her to approach the podium and accept the plaque.

She had not prepared an acceptance speech, choosing to act in the manner that had become her trademark: winging it.

"I am grateful to my colleagues at the academy for this honor, grateful for being awarded for simply doing what I love doing. What I have always been called to do."

Snook glanced at the young people in the audience. "Most of all, I am grateful to my students. No matter how old and mature you think you are, you are youthful."

Audience members chuckled. Senior faculty members glimpsed at one another and nodded.

"I look into your beautiful, youthful faces, and I espy your burning call to rescue and protect our planet. Much like I ... like I was called upon so long ago. That fire in your young bellies keeps we seniors going."

Snook smiled and nodded at random colleagues from UNC and around the country. "And thank you to my generous, talented colleagues who day in and day out exude passion in searching for scientific truths."

Snook stared at her plaque for a moment, and then back at her audience. "Passion fuels our drive to challenge what was believed for thousands of years to be truth. Passion fuels our drive to seek truth in what has been wrongly declared to be magic or fantasy or absurdity."

For a moment, Snook shut her eyes to search inside herself. "Our drive is far more than passion, isn't it? It's a necessity. When we are on track, nothing adverse or disbelieving or challenging diverts us."

She paused long enough that silence became uncomfortable for her audience.

"Where do wild, non-conforming, creative ideas of ours originate? Do they pop into our heads? Come from unseen forces reaching into us?" She turned to colleagues sitting behind her. "Ideas in music, in art, in dance, in math or science ... we are blessed those ideas flow like flooding rivers into us and from us."

She returned to her audience. "Our creativity is a most private matter. Attempts to describe that creativity with words? Even poets fail.

In the end, we are gifted to see and hear not only what is around us, but what lives inside us. That treasure informs our duty. Informs our missions. And we share— goodness gracious how we share the fruits of our creativity. We never allow anyone or anything to silence us or thwart our relentless search for truths of our universe."

Snook stared inside audience members, checking if her words landed and stuck.

"Bless all of you. You are in my heart."

She pressed the plaque to her chest and returned to her stage seat.

Sounds from a standing ovation filled the room—filled her soul.

Once the presentation concluded and she had shaken an abundance of hands, and once the great university hall had almost emptied and she was surrounded by her husband, children, and grandchildren, she led her family up the aisle toward the hall's front door.

A man standing in the doorway had his eyes locked on her face. He was clearly waiting for her.

As she neared, the man smiled. His smile felt familiar, and yet, she could not recall ever having seen him.

The man was holding a small, plain paper bag with paper handles—obviously a gift bag.

He stepped toward her. "Dr. Frederick. I am a grateful follower of your work. I have read all your papers and use your ideas and findings in my own teaching."

Snook reached out and shook his hand. "That is very kind. Where do you teach? What is your name?"

"West Virginia University. The Department of Civil and Environmental Engineering graduate programs."

"Wonderful. I know your chairperson from years of conferences. You have a wonderful program."

The man lifted the bag and gently handed it to her. "A thank-you gift for all you have done—in addition to your well-earned award." The man winked.

Snook appeared grateful and perplexed, looking to family members who appeared equally baffled.

The man nodded in a highly gentleman-like manner and departed.

Snook's fourteen-year-old granddaughter frowned. "Well, that was weird."

Her five-year-old grandson tried to peek in the bag. "What is it?"

Snook peered into the bag, panicked, hurriedly stepped outside, and scanned the campus grounds.

The man had vanished.

Her family joined her outside with her grandson still demanding an answer. "What's in the bag?"

Snook pulled out a blue, red, and white bag of "Fun Size" Baby Ruths.

Her granddaughter rolled her eyes. "Now that's really really weird."

Snook chuckled as her eyes teared. "Isn't it? Baby Ruths."

"That's just dumb."

Snook retrieved a small white box from the gift bag and stared at it, feeling puzzled and a bit apprehensive.

Her grandson's hand seemed to have a mind of its own, stretching toward the gift. "Open it."

Snook slowly opened the box and pulled out a necklace with a pendant. A card in the box simply read, *Thanks Snook.*

Scrutinizing the gift, her granddaughter wrinkled her face. "Yuk. That thing's old and disgusting."

Snook rubbed her finger over tarnished metal and burn marks. She turned the pendant over. Engraved words were disfigured but she was able to make out two words: *Love Frederik.*

Snook sat outside on the hall's marble steps, ignoring her family's whispers while she transported back in time.

Friendship between an eight-year-old girl and a seven-year-old boy. Exploring woods together. Napping together in a tree palace. Keeping secrets. Surviving murderous adults. Being labeled as misfits. Living in a time when all that was necessary for happiness was a ragged backpack or a Baby Ruth.

Snook's grandson tapped her shoulder. "Can we go now?"

Snook turned to him. "Of course we can. I'm hungry. What about the rest of you?"

The five-year-old tugged at her again. "Can I have a candy bar first?"

Snook laughed. "Of course you can." She tore open the bag. "Here you go. Pass the bag around. All of you take one. I haven't seen this candy in … in a really long time."

DC Fidler (Author)

A native of the North Carolina Appalachian Mountains, DC Fidler lives in Charlotte, North Carolina.

He has combined a career in academic psychiatry and cultural psychiatry with a lifetime of playwriting, acting, directing, composing music, and teaching creative writing and the dramatic arts.

He is an award-winning playwright, author of the textbook: *Psychiatry for Actors: Building a Character Using Psychiatric Principles*, author of short stories, author of novels: *Boogieban, Wood Whisperers, Dangerous Art*, and co-author with RJ Casey of the novel: *Green Lights of Baghdad*.

Plays, Novels, and Textbooks by DC Fidler

Novels and Textbooks
- Boogieban
- Wood Whisperers
- Dangerous Art
- Green Lights of Baghdad (With RJ Casey)
- Psychiatry for Actors: Building a Character Using Psychiatric Principles

Plays
- Voices in the Woods
- Guilt by Association (With RJ Casey)
- Three Diaries
- Sir William Bowlinggreen and Company
- Shiraz
- Anniversary of Miss Nanette Pringle (With RJ Casey)
- School Children Hiding Under Desks
- Grams
- Camp Uni
- Boogieban: Two-Actor Script (With RJ Casey)
- Boogieban: Seven-Actor Version
- Ahulaqs
- Elk and Wolf (With Travis Teffner)
- Santee Delta (With Travis Teffner)
- Celtic Crossing
- Stone Touchin'
- Daugherty Park Merry-Go-Round
- La Dynastie
- The Last Farm
- Gyges
- Begat
- Hijacked Lives
- Five X

Short Plays
- Persons
- Cruise
- Mobile to Where
- Oman Truce
- Second Amendment
- The Greek God Club
- Microscopic Misconceptions
- Drone Guns
- Moon Bugs (With Travis Teffner)

Screenplays
- Green Lights of Baghdad (with RJ Casey and Matt Westbrook)

Short Stories and Novelettes
- Recipient
- The Dust Portal
- Charon: A Modern Myth
- Time Will Tell
- Snook

Musicals
- Pied Piper (With Lauren Horacek)
- Healer Man
- Medicine Show